Nunatak

Nunatak

Garrett Buhl Robinson

ISBN: 1469962780
ISBN-13: 978 1469962788

This book is dedicated to those who love with all they are, even when they are not loved in return.

Your love is not in vain.

My life dangles from a rail above the boiling water. The propellers churn the frothing chaos, pushing the massive ferry through the interior passage along the Pacific Coast of Canada. My thoughts crumble and fall into this tiny disturbance of a vast sea as the wake fades into the indifferent distance.

There are no stars; none that may twinkle in my eyes. The ceiling of indistinct clouds is a fuzzy blur dimly lit by the flicker of this buoyant bulb of a boat with a frail wire of filament delicately stretched between the prow and stern.

The islands to the west and the entire continent of North America to the east are completely concealed in a fathomless night. There are no signs of life I can recognize. There are no towns or houses. There is no development. There are no lamps lined along smoothly paved streets. There are no windows with angular frames glowing with settled and domestic warmth. There is no civilization beyond the rails of this vessel and the splash of this wake that quickly dissipates into the frigid pulse of waves. This boat carries a lonely spark into a primordial dark.

In the indistinguishable distance, two eyes open. They are eyes I have gazed deep inside where my bleary sight has touched a kindness sweeter than any life I have ever known. I can see their image fluttering adorably, delicately flashing with astonishing beauty. Those eyes dispel the darkness. Those eyes see me through the night. Connie's eyes.

The roar of the wake fades and I hear her voice. She tells me she will go with me. She tells me she will not leave me. She loves me.

So what did I do? I left without her. I told her I would be back. I told her I wanted to marry her. I asked her to marry me, but I didn't have a ring. I didn't have anything but a promise and the vacancy of my departure.

Of course she wouldn't say yes. Not then. Not while I stuffed clothes in my duffle. She's a woman. She's heard promises all her life: extravagant promises, earnest promises, desperate promises, tender promises, weeping promises, rhapsodic promises, promises of fanciful grandeur, promises of devoted adoration, promises of amorous magnificence, promises of gallant reliance, promises of every imaginable form and fashion that would always open into the emptiness of betrayal and abandon. If she says "yes" to the attention she deserves, she is cheapened by agreement. If she says "no," she is scorned for coldness. She is a woman, and this woman, Constance, is wise. She said she would give me her answer when I return.

For once, I found someone who truly loves me. Through my life the most I could hope to find in others is tolerance, but in her I found kindness and acceptance. She embraces me. She smiles at the sight of me. She opens her arms to me. She reaches for me, leans on me, bolsters me.

2

Nunatak

She enriches me. In her I found love, her love, but not my own.

I've always heard if you're not sure whether you love someone or not, then you don't. Love is something where there is no doubt. But with all she gives me, all the attention, all the affection, all the patience, if I feel nothing with this, with this abundance, with this profusion of beauty she pours forth, maybe I am incapable of feeling anything. She loves me, truly loves me and through my long, lonely life, that is more than I've ever had before. Isn't that enough? What makes me think I could ever find more? What makes me think I deserve more?

I try rationalizing. I begin tabulating the benefits of the relationship. She gives me comfort. She gives me stability. She gives me refreshment. She gives me joy, at least what I am capable of receiving. She gives me life. But this disgusts me. Are my only desires what she gives me? Is even the thought of pleasing her simply a means by which I may gloat over my own capacity, virility and generosity? What do I have to offer her? I have so little. I have practically nothing. I have only myself. But that is all she has ever asked for.

When we last spoke, and all the anxious days before I told her I was leaving, I expected to return. I was determined to return. Now, embarked on the open sea, surrounded by the untamed wilderness, I feel free. I feel relieved and released. I feel nothing.

The railing numbly trembles with the diesel engine. Overhead sooty smoke billows from the stack. My thoughts slip beneath the riveted steel plates of the boat. I enter the engine room. The mechanics yell over the restless rumble of the throttled engine. Their ears are muffed from the relentless commotion. Shafts extend from the engine and twist into holes in the hull to turn propellers that drive the ferry through the thick liquid of the sea. The whole craft is built for stability, for a smooth passage, for the comfort of the passengers and the safety of the journey. And to accomplish this, firmly mounted inside a steel encasement is this roaring, raging engine driving inside to whirl the blades of the screws.

With the heels of my hands, I push myself up from the rail and turn to walk away from the wake. Opening a door, I step inside the lounge where people sprawl in the seats and on the floor as they sleep beneath dimmed lights. There are cabins in the ferry for a considerably higher priced ticket, but these are the cheap seats where one sits and sleeps where one pleases, at least within reason. The door closes behind me with a suctioned seal. There is the faint sound of the sea sloshing and slapping against the hull. There is the humming of the engine. There is a general buzz inside. The buzz permeates through me as it does the whole boat and all it contains. I find a space on the floor, unstuff my bag, crawl into my sack, squirm for a minute as I flatten a side of my body to the floor and then resting my head on a pile of my laundry, I thoughtlessly sink into sleep.

2

My morning begins with my awakening amongst the polite whispers of others gathering and bundling their sleeping things. The diffused light of the hazy day passes through the large observatory windows of the lounge. Through the night, and through my oblivious slumber, the boat has continued the course.

Slipping out of my bed roll, I quickly stuff everything back into my bag. My sprawl neatly packs into the bulge of the duffle I cinch to a close with the clinched teeth of the zipper. Standing, I pause to steady myself upon the swaying rock of the boat laboring through the waves.

There are showers at the aft deck, but I am not expecting to stay completely fresh for the three day voyage. I'm heading to work in a cannery for the summer. There is little need to prim myself in preparation of meeting a pool of dead fish.

I walk to the bow of the boat to see what lies ahead, but the wind is fierce and the air is cold and damp. I turn my head and my thoughts tumble downwind. I decide the stern, where I stood last night, would be a bit more sheltered.

Walking along the side of the boat, strolling with the passing of the water below, I watch the slow drift of the jagged land. The islands are the coastal range of mountains partially immersed in the Pacific Ocean. From their heights, capped with the low ceiling of clouds, thick evergreens march down the steep slopes till their roots are exposed at the shore, gripping and clutching the ground gnawed by the relentless sea.

This is the Alaskan Marine Highway, a navigable waterway that winds between the islands that provide shelter from the open ocean. Why it is called a highway is beyond me. First, it's at sea level. Second, there are no road signs. There isn't even a single billboard and if there was, what would it advertise, life preservers? The thought is absurd. For that matter, here, thought itself is absurd. There is only the resolve to endure. Beyond the ridge that crests somewhere in the clouds there is a vast, trackless wilderness and if I stumbled over that edge, I wouldn't see a sign of civilization, not even a beer can left by poachers, for hundreds of the most rugged miles.

Coming from the city, I am accustomed to being imbedded in the arrangements of being human. The pathways are paved for transportation. The slopes are etched with steps. The vertical surfaces are plastered with expressions that advertise the satisfaction of every imaginable need. Even the night sky glows amber with the burning urges of never ending busyness. At every turn, overhead and underfoot, everything is designed and fabricated by the human mind with little more than humans in mind. Even the air is a mechanically conditioned breeze.

Here, there are no deliveries. There are no direct routes from house to house. There is no metered electricity.

Nunatak

There are no channels of programs. There are no compartmental spaces or revolving doors. There are no beams of riveted steel framing corridors where only birds had passed before. I see one rock, a huge boulder that had rolled from the ridge of the mountain to rest momentarily at the shore. That rock has probably been sitting in that same place, set in that same position, since before we began numbering sheaves of wheat with cuneiform on soft clay tablets as those accumulating counts began figuring into the epic steps of Gilgamesh. Upon these undulating slopes the trees grow where their seeds have fallen and take root where they sprout and stalk into the sunlight they find, or they don't and they die. If I was to step onto one of those shores and try finding my way, I would be in little less desperate of a situation than if I had been dropped in the middle of the ocean.

At the stern, people crowd on the deck. We pass a small sailboat and I feel some comfort in recognizing a fellow traveller, like bumping into someone from my home state while visiting a foreign place and either enjoying or avoiding the affinity as I recognize the relatable and see portions of myself in another.

Watching the sailboat fitfully pitch over the widening fan of the ferry's wake, I notice the dorsal fin of a killer whale rise through the surface. Knowing that many take this trip to spot the wildlife and not sensing an excited stir in the crowd to indicate anyone else had spotted the oceanic mammal, I burst out, "Orca!"

I feel silly shouting. After all, the dorsal fin has disappeared beneath the surface by now. I feel like an upstart crow or some pseudo-whaler shouting "Thar she blows", setting a racket of peg legged jolly rogers clacking across the deck, lifting their eye patches to search with a vengeance for something they missed.

A bunch of kids begin tugging at my sleeve urgently asking, "Where?" I suppose they show more sense than the adults who seem convinced they can spot the whale on their own, but still, I don't like kids. They remind me how helpless we all really are.

"Look toward the sailboat." I tell them, fortunate to have some discernable marker for direction. Except for the artificial and arbitrary, there are no landmarks. Direction is just another plot through the distinct fiction of our lives. The only distinguishing feature of the wilderness is that it is indistinguishable.

The kids immediately turn from me, probably forgetting my entire existence, directing their attention toward something entirely new, retaining nothing more than the faint expression of direction, "look toward the sailboat." Many of the grown-ups heard the instructions too and everyone seems to be beaming with anticipation. Then the anxiety arises. The question of disappointing doubt creeps into everyone's mind. They wonder if they have been duped. I begin to wonder myself. Did I really see the dorsal fin? Am I just seeing things? Was it just another mirage like every image?

After all, I know I don't see the world as it is, I only see the world as I am open to perceive it, as I am capable of comprehending it, as I dimly expect it and reluctantly accept it.

Then suddenly, to everyone's delight, the whale breaks into the open again. The dorsal juts through the seas' surface and a cloud of condensed breath is released before the whale pulls a gulp of the sky back into the plunging deep with the arching dive of its sleek body.

People squeal with delight and begin asking one another, "Did you see it?" as if trying to dispel the persistent doubt between themselves, reassuring one another of the monumental event they had witnessed together in this lonely sea and wilderness.

I retreat from the deck and step back inside the lounge. I take a seat. The cushion bulges and balloons beneath my weight and then slowly wheezes with the release of air as the padding collapses. It was a solitary Orca; one without a pod; one that wanders forever in an ocean without end, like an albatross that can never land.

The overhead speaker crackles to life. "Hello everyone. This is your captain speaking. We are about to sail into the open waters. This is one section of the cruise that is not sheltered by the westward islands, so the water will get a little rough. We are expecting some moderate swells of about five feet. For your own safety, the crew asks you to please keep a firm grasp of the railings when walking around."

I know you can't hear the voice, only read the script that is written upon the indistinct space between us, but are you surprised when I tell you the voice of the captain is the voice of a woman? Well, on this voyage it is. Many associate a woman's voice with maternity, brooding over each concern and fussing with every consideration, more inclusive than divisive, more protective than decisive. I always try to remind myself that there are far more dispositions of character than can be defined by two genders.

3

Waiting for the cafeteria to open for lunch, I find myself wandering around the boat. The cold, damp wind buffets against me and I run across a little nook where I am tempted to stoop inside for shelter. I see someone has already found the space, but there's plenty of room for two and I think it might be nice to have some company, even if we let the howling wind do all the talking.

"Do you mind if I have a seat?"

His arm limply gestures over the open space as if feebly flicking its availability to me.

Taking the seat, I ask some of the expected questions: where he's from, what he does. He slowly ponders each response. Basic communication seems to be a challenge for him. He struggles with each word and arduously pieces together the simplest sentences. I begin to grow impatient as I wait for him to fumble through his clumsy assembly of each alphabet block statement.

Persisting in my search for some relatable topic, some shared interest upon which we may converse, I ask where he is going and am astonished with his response. I repeat it back to make sure I heard him right, "You're going to Nunatak?"

"Yea."

"Me too." He doesn't react as if he is extremely impressed with this coincidence but I am hoping to find some insight. All I know about the place is that I am scheduled to show up on a specific date to register for work, so I hope to pry out some more information, "What are you doing there?"

"Cannery work."

"Really, where at?"

"Glacier..." Then he pauses seemingly to build his momentum to surmount the impossible feat of pronouncing two consecutive polysyllable words, "Glacier Fishing." He finally fumbles out.

"Wow. Me too." He still doesn't seem to recognize the magnitude of this incredible coincidence and I wonder if he is about to drop off to sleep or something, so I hop around as I talk, hoping to retain his attention. "What's your name?"

"Tuesday."

"Tuesday? Really? Like the day of the week?"

"Yea. There's only one Tuesday a week, but I'm Tuesday all the time."

Obviously, the effortless ease by which he recites this indicates it is his stock phrase. I remain skeptical. "That's not some street name is it? I learned a long time ago never to trust anyone who doesn't use their real name."

"No. It's my real name. Tuesday Paz."

"Oh. I'm Evan Moore. Have you worked at Glacier before?"

"Yea. Once. Last year." He says, haltingly.

"Want to get some lunch?"

"No. I'm fasting.... Cleansing."

"Fasting? What are you a monk? The cannery business is hard work isn't it? Wouldn't you want to have all your strength when you arrive?"

"Sure, but it's just how it is." Tuesday slurs each word.

"What do mean? Don't you have any money?"

"Not now. I spent it on the ticket up here."

"Well, fasting's great, but tell me, if you had any money, would you be eating lunch?"

I corner him with the question and he pauses, apparently searching for a way to evade, yet is too exhausted to pursue it. I am beginning to suspect that he only mentioned fasting to give me an excuse from feeling obligated to help him. Then again, it could be a clever trick.

He finally confesses, "Yea, probably."

"Well how about I buy you lunch. It sucks not having food. Fasting because you want to is one thing. But fasting because you have to is something else entirely. I call it starving. Come on. Let's get something to eat. You can pay me back when we get our first check."

He graciously accepts.

While we shuffle through the cafeteria line, I let Tuesday know he can order what he wants. There's no reason for him to hold back. If he's hungry, he needs to eat. At the table, he takes a big bite from the hamburger. There is an ecstatic expression on his face as he chews. I can see the lights brighten in his eyes. His body is already recognizing it is being fed and I wonder how long he has gone without eating.

For the next few minutes, I remain quiet, not wanting to disturb his obvious enjoyment. It is a simple meal, but even muddy water is sweet to a parched throat.

As we begin to talk over what little is left on our plates, I mention a dream I had the previous night. The severity of my recent departure must have distorted my thoughts to unsettle my sleep. I don't pursue it though. The topic is a faux pas. Mentioning personal dreams in a casual conversation is like talking about friends that no one else knows. To my surprise though, Tuesday seizes upon the topic.

"Dreams are fascinating, not just on a personal basis, but in general. They may seem to have a mystical element to them, but I believe they have an obvious and easily explained utility. They are simply the most effective means for the mental organization of information. Through each day, we accumulate information as experience. Then we apply this experience in similar situations to conduct our lives most efficiently and effectively. Dreams are an organization of information that corresponds with our sensory experience with the world. They are simply our minds invoking a fantastic experience of our lives so new information may be installed where it most likely will be needed.

"It's similar to how we organize our lives by storing forks and knives in the kitchen, hairdryers in the bathroom and wrenches in the garage. We store these tools where we use them."

The meal has certainly done Tuesday good. In fact, he appears completely transformed. Where before he was staggering like a hobbled horse, now he is racing like a thoroughbred. Before I get a word in edgewise, he gallops along:

"The fact that our dreams are primarily visual is no surprise either. Our perception of the world is primarily visual. In contemporary times, even the flavors we taste and the perfumes we smell are introduced to us through visual marketing. I would say that my own dreams are 90% visual, 5% audio, and the remaining 5% are divided between touch, taste, smell and various other senses."

I have to pull back at the reigns here, "Whoa, hold on there. Various others? What other senses do we have? What do you mean, 'Extra-Sensory Perception?'"

"I don't mean 'ESP' as most people would consider it such as clairvoyance, prescience, and the such, but the notion that we only have five senses is outrageous. Everyone knows we have more than five senses, whether they admit it or not. What about our sense of equilibrium? That's a sense. It is a sense of our orientation to the draw of gravity that is measured in our inner ear. There is the sense of proprioception, which is our sense of the position of our body in space. If we didn't have this sense, believe me, we would be knocking over glasses and tripping over chairs, and committing who knows what other bumptious behavior.

"These are just some of the obvious ones, but there are a number of others which are much more subtle and have arisen through cultural interaction. What about our sense of decorum and discretion? People may say these are simply a matter of tradition and social propriety, but they certainly allow us to navigate our lives through various social situations with whatever grace and delicacy our sense is refined to recognize. Even language is a sense. In some ways it is almost like echolocation that provides us with an awareness of the contents of other's thoughts. It wasn't until recently that we discovered birds are able to sense the earth's magnetic field to direct their migrations. Of course we can sense the magnetic field too, but we use a compass. In that, our ingenuity has become the most powerful evolutionary mechanism as we broaden our senses and extend our appendages with our inventions."

As intriguing as Tuesday's discourse is, my eyes wander to a nearby table to see a man fidgeting with a napkin dispenser. I can almost see his ears sharpen to points as he subtly twitches in the rhythm of Tuesday's statements. As Tuesday winds to a conclusion, the man lopes toward us. He approaches with a stern, even fierce, determination and his face is tensed in a snarl. The man approaches Tuesday from behind and leans into his ear with a reddened expression and hollers, "Wrong!" before stomping off.

Nunatak

With the furious rebuke of the stranger, Tuesday cringes. As he ate, his life appeared to bloom beautifully and every petal of his thoughts unfolded in the most extravagant way, and now he appeared to wither in a scathing instant.

"Do you know that guy?" I ask.

"Who?"

"That guy who just walked by and yelled in your ear?" I pivot in my seat to try spotting him, but he is gone.

"I have no idea who you're talking about. I don't know anybody. You, just like everybody else, have seen me before. I'm the one who is always alone."

This sounds extremely suspicious to me. Tuesday is obviously evading the question and I insist upon an answer. "But that person seemed to have a personal vendetta against you. I know you heard him. I saw you flinch when he yelled."

Tuesday reluctantly confesses, "Well, you see, there was something I did a long time ago that seems to have infuriated everybody and people will probably never forgive me."

Hearing this, I sit for a moment in silent expectation. He has confessed, but he has admitted nothing. I expect him to explain what this terrible offense was. Instead, his attention is redirected to what few morsels of food remain on his plate and he rubs one last French-Fry to mop up every last grain of salt. The suspense is killing me though and I ask, "Which was...? What did you do?"

Tuesday looks up with an expression of complete astonishment, amazed that I don't know. Finally, with a bruised quietus, he says, "I was born."

4

The next day we arrive at a port. The stop is unremarkable. The town may have a permanent population of only a few hundred people. As we launch, the boat does not career toward the next destination as expected. Instead, we linger about a quarter mile from the dock. A few fishing boats sit in the distance, but it is difficult to judge their size. There are surrounding islands, but the magnitude of the space is difficult to scale.

From the speaker, there is an announcement, "Folks, this is your captain. You all have probably noticed we are experiencing a delay in our departure. A crabbing vessel has capsized nearby and a few members of the crew are reported missing. We have been asked to assist in the search. We ask that everyone keep a look out for any crew members in the water. The accident occurred off our starboard side at a distance of about 2 miles. For those of you who do not know, the starboard side of the ship is to the right if you are facing forward."

With the announcement, a large portion of the passengers shift to the starboard side of the boat. I can hear a few people speaking with one another about retrieving their binoculars. Everyone wants to help although no one is really sure what they can do or what they are looking for.

There is a frenzy in finding the crew, and understandably so. This is not quite the Bearing Sea, but this water is still frigid and a person wouldn't last long. Hypothermia sets in after a few minutes and as the body's core cools, every light of the life quickly fades until it is completely snuffed. Local fishers race toward the bellied up boat. They know it could have been anyone of them, and in fact, it is. Even the swiftest Coast Guard helicopter won't be here for several hours. They have few resources to rely upon except one another.

I hear someone explaining nearby, "It's a small crabbing boat. They set their traps at the sea floor and attach them to buoys. Later they come wench them up. Sometimes a trap will snag on the bottom and the wench can flip one of these small boats right over. That's probably what happened."

The ferry boat drifts through the water. There is little more we can do. The ferry is too big to approach any closer. We vigilantly search over the riffling water, each white cap is a flash of hope that quickly vanishes and turns to nothing.

After about an hour, I hear the speaker again. "Folks, this is your captain. We have word that they have recovered two members of the crew, but a third is still missing. I just spoke with the Coast Guard and they want us to resume our course. We thank everyone for their help in the search and we all hope the best for the third remaining crew member." Then, abruptly, the crackling speaker cuts off.

I hear someone state in a gruff and somber voice, "He's gone. No one can last that long in this water."

Nunatak

A man beside me wearing a weathered baseball cap with an anchor stitched on the front panel blows a bitter rasp of smoke and resentfully tosses a cigarette over the rail. The deck is probably fifty feet above the water. I watch the butt tumble through the air. There is a faint looping ribbon of smoke trailing from the smoldering ember that immediately extinguishes upon contact with the sea. There is no sizzle that I hear. There is no more smoke. There is just a pallid tip of the filter floating on the surface as the ferry slips away. A cigarette can be a lot like death, in fact, it is death for too many, a slow and excruciatingly painful death, but life has to be more than a smoke.

Garrett Buhl Robinson

5

Late the next day the first signs of a settlement appear as a refreshing anomaly in the wilderness of mountains and sea. As the boat slowly follows a narrow strait, angular boxes of houses appear in the mist like mysterious bubbles rising to the surface of the sea. The houses were probably built with the lumber of the cleared lots where they stand. As few more buildings appear, my eyes trace a dirt road tying them together. The two parallel lines of exposed ground make muddy ribbons over the wavy terrain.

Around a bend, floating docks fan their fingers through the cove where the fishing boats bob on the water and gently tug the ropes that tie them down. Their keels gracefully arch into the emerald sea. Some of the cabins are lit. A solitary clatter of tin pans tumbles over the water. A curious face peeks through a portal before the gentle wake of the ferry ripples to the sleeping hulls that nod into a softly settling sway.

A massive dock appears. Thick, barnacled posts firmly stand in the sloshing water as I see a scramble of hands ready to catch the approaching boat. There is a bright building broadly painted with the names, "Nunatak, Alaska, USA." Reluctantly, the tiny town appears in the background. First the rainbow coronas of the streetlamps spike their light through the thick, wet air, then store fronts and surrounding houses shyly and discretely peak out from obscurity. I am not sure if the town awakes with the arrival of the ferry, but it seems to stir in its sleep. It is nearly midnight, and dusk has dimmed the sky. The drizzle wafts in the wind. Here, all the elements appear to move without hindrance, and despite the obvious exposure, the town stays snuggled in a bundle, quaint and comfortable. I hear someone explain, "The only time it stops raining here, is when it snows."

The engines rev to slow the boat's drifting momentum. I see the stir of the water welt to the surface at the side of the boat as the propellers reverse. Thin lines are tossed to the dock, trailing behind the monkey fists knotted at the ends. The dock hands catch the draping arch of the whimsical strings, then rapidly pull in the thickening rope to tie the boat to the dock. The dock's timber groans and creaks as it catches the ferry and holds.

Whirling my arm to twist my bag over my shoulder, I step in line to disembark. A boon lowers as a bridge. There is the sound of metal latching and locking in place. A member of the crew swings open a section of the railing. The line trickles down the ramp.

From the advantage of the boat's height, I can see a van in the parking lot with "Glacier Fishing" painted on the side. I suppose the company wants to make sure we get settled in directly, otherwise some people might wander off to the closest bar and get lost in alcohol. Stepping onto firm land is odd as my body still tries to adjust to the rising and falling of the deck. I suppose Tuesday would say that during the short boat ride, I had developed a sense of the sea. This makes me wonder how it would feel if the planet suddenly stopped spinning. Everyone might suddenly fall over, all at the same time, all in the same direction.

Greeting the driver of the van, I toss my bag in the back and wait. Tuesday appears and I wave him over. As the line of disembarking passengers disperses, it is interesting to see some people I recognize from the journey gathering. Others are greeted by family or friends and load their bags in cars and pick-up trucks.

They all have their places to go, places to return after the day to day ventures extending out to fulfill obligations and closing the circuit of their journeys with the day's earnings in their bundled arms. I envision imaginary homes curled around hearths, firm with reassuring security, interiors embellished with the occupant's interests, filled with their enjoyment and soothed with their rest and repose as they pause to revitalize their lives. Others may be stretched out in the furthest lengths of one of their loops, venturing into the wild for the invigoration of robust enjoyment, wishing to peer into the immense vistas offered at civilization's edge. Some others may be students returning home for the summer as they notch through the increments extending out on their own, climbing the steps of intellectual development as professors guide them in tours through the tranquil towers and palaces of ideas.

I feel my life loop too, but it loops in a spiral, either a vortex or a vertex, as I am always turning away.

6

Arriving at the site, there are the typical procedures of processing. I am identified and pass through certain checks. I answer questions and am inspected. Then I am handed bags of linens and a pillow, given keys to the dorm and told the number of my assigned bunk. Then I sign some papers and I'm off. I wonder if this is similar to how the salmon arrive on the boats too.

I walk from the residential office and laundry to a three story block building. The cafeteria is on the first floor. In the window I see the schedule and breakfast is between 7 to 8. The dormitory rooms are stacked above. On the third floor, I open the door into a large, cubical room. A red bulb lights the interior. No one is around or everyone is asleep so I feel safe to assume I didn't stumble into a rave party. Too bad I didn't bring any black light posters, if I actually had any. The red light must stay on through the night not to hurt any groggy eyes. I assume the other rooms are the same. The design is cinderblock austere. It is built for storage and sleep. It is secure. It is dry. It is warm. It is occupied. It serves its purpose. There are no architectural frills for aesthetics. Here, the beauty most desired is simply to survive.

There are twelve bunks arranged in three groups. They are not what I had anticipated. I was expecting bare bone bunks made of steel pipe with a lumpy mattress on a squeaky flat spring that would hammock beneath my weight into waking backaches. However, this company actually makes effort to provide the workers with some supportive comfort. The bunks are completely enclosed with wood walls with the exception of one side which provides access. This open side has a curtain for privacy. I find the one labeled with the number I was assigned. The key works and I cram my stuff into a drawer. I make the bed and crawl inside. There is an overhead light in the compartment. I draw the curtain and lean back against my pillow. There are some scratched names as previous residents felt compelled to leave their mark in the different ways they spell "fidgety boredom." It's not really like the inside of a can, but it might have a resemblance to a coffin. Perhaps I have finally found my place and my place is in a grave.

I pull out my book and return to Camus' *The Myth of Sisyphus*. I never realized until now how the lines of text resemble the fish ladders that are built around dams so salmon can ascend the rivers. I pour my attention over the contents to see what ideas take shape and surge through my thoughts, coursing through the passages, leaping over the fluttering pages, and spawning in contemplative pools until weariness releases me into sleep.

7

The next morning I sleep late. I don't rise until after nine. Stepping outside onto the landing of the steps, I notice the expansive view. Beyond the docks, across the strait, I see the mountains of the surrounding islands rise into the clouds. The cloud ceiling appears so low and close, I feel I can reach up and comb my fingers through the mist.

On the strait, a white dander is scattered over the water. I hear a motor throttle and see a pontoon plane straighten in a line to launch. It builds speed and begins to lighten its load from the floats that skip and skim across the water as the weight is shifted to the wings carried with the lift of rushing air as the plane is propped into the atmosphere. What I thought was dander, turns out to be thousands of sea birds. As the plane flies by, they whirl into flight like a wake in the air, before relaxing back to bobble on the water.

The sight of the plane allows me to gauge the dimensions of the area, yet it is still difficult to grasp the distance of the surrounding islands. I try to sight a single tree, but all I can see are blurring blotches of shades of green. My eyes follow the creases on the mountain sides, envisioning the rivulets that run within them, accumulating in confluents gathered from the rainy sky, cascading over mossy stones until they splash onto the reedy alluvium and meander through time to pour into the sloshing turns of the tide. After the moisture rises from the ocean, it is pressed against the coastal mountains. As the air is pushed up over the ridges and peaks, it cools in the higher elevations and the moisture condenses into droplets that become too heavy for the updrafts to carry. So it rains without end as if the Pacific Ocean was tipped to pour exhaustlessly over these steep mountain sides that bristle with vibrant life.

The Glacial Fisheries processing complex sprawls below, nimbly stepping out over the water on the stilted legs of docks to receive the meat of the sea from unloading boats. The facility is a garbled mass of buildings, each stemming along pathways and pipes from the modest, original structure, like an embryo gestating, dividing and multiplying in a diversifying arrangement of a singular organism. Wisps of steam rise from the refrigerant units. Occasionally clashes of sheet metal escape from somewhere in the interior. The place is alive with the people and machines working inside.

At the bottom of the steps, I see the cafeteria is closed. A few people are working, wiping tables, straightening containers, stewing the contents of big pots on the stove's blazing eyes. Besides this, the space of the cafeteria that immediately interest me, not the place where the food is prepared or served, but where the food is eaten, is vacant. The empty tables and chairs are flossed with a single swab of a mop that only pauses for a ringing in the bucket. Still, ignoring the obvious, I tug at the door. The brief gap of slack snaps with a rattling commotion. The people inside look up and point at the watches on their wrists and then shake their heads as if trying to dislodge their thoughts from my disappointing disruption. Of course, I was only hoping to get a cup of coffee. I wasn't expecting a specially catered meal, but obviously this is not the local cafe. I work in their schedule. They do not work in mine.

I notice another building nearby. Beneath the cover of what appears to have been a carport, I see people huddled outside. Tuesday is sitting on a concrete curb watching a game of chess. I greet him and sit nearby.

"Do you play chess Tuesday?"

"Not really, or at least not very well so that I could interest myself or anyone else, but the game is fascinating. It's like watching a kind of conversation."

Honestly, this was plenty of information for which I could sit and contemplate the game from a completely new perspective. I had always associated conversations with talking, but never considered the alternating moves of chess as a type of dialog. However, Tuesday continues:

"It has its own vocabulary, syntax, everything. There are various pieces with their own identities, references and relations. In ways, you can even sense the characteristic movements of the pieces with the unsurpassable versatility of the queen, the encumbered steps of the king, the obliquities of the bishops, the surprise flanking flight of the knights, the difficult release of the rooks and the slow steady march of the pawns.

"What boggles my mind is how a great player has a true feel of the game. Most players, even good players, see the game as individual threads of each move, or how they can stitch strategies together with series of moves. It is a jumbled ball of thread two people try to untangle by tugging it from one another. But a great player sees a tapestry in the patterns of possibilities that cover the entire board and change shape with every layer of each alternating turn."

"Sounds like a very complicated way to look at the game." Sadly, the only response to this elaborate explanation I can come up with seems to be blunt skepticism, as if my thoughts are too obtuse to penetrate the intricacies of Tuesday's considerations.

"No, it is just my feeble attempt at an explanation of a truly astonishing process that some people can accomplish with no more difficulty than stirring cream into coffee," Suddenly, Tuesday's tone becomes ebullient which cues me to expect another surging surprise of ideas, "but have you ever watched how the cream disperses into a cup of coffee? Have you ever noticed the curls eddy like a Mandelbrot pattern? It is practically an infinite recursion whirling down to individual atoms. My description may sound incredibly elaborate but every one of us accomplishes truly miraculous feats even by lifting a finger or uttering a single sentence that others may comprehend, which I might add is one task where I can be severely challenged." Then he pauses for a moment to consider this, perhaps searching for a way to resolve the problem, as if trying to understand what boggles him about himself, so that he may avoid boggling others. "Did you know that there are over 300 trillion different moves that can be played in just the first four turns of a chess game?"

"And has anyone made them all?"

"Not yet. We're not even close. The human species hasn't even played a total of 300 trillion games. In fact, our species has not even existed for 300 trillion seconds, and we will most probably evolve into something else before that entire lapse of time has passed. Anyway, most of these sequences would have little strategic value, at least for winning a game. But what I find fascinating…."

"But it sounds like you find everything fascinating, Tuesday." I interject, not as much trying to disrupt Tuesday's flow of thought, but to give my scrambling attention a chance to catch up.

Tuesday quirks his head a bit to consider this and then looks at me in that blank expression of astonishment I have seen on his face so many times already, "Well, yea, of course. Everything is," then he pauses for a moment and before clarifying, "and far more." Then he launches again, "But in regards to this, even though there may be more ways to play a game of chess than there are particles in the universe, there is one specific number and only one specific number of different games and we can determine what that number is before we can play them. And all this can be accomplished with little more than a single plane with 64 spaces, 32 pieces and a handful rules by which to play. It is a quantity of possibilities that populates more multiply than the exponential. And this is only a few characteristics of the unfathomably elaborate elegance of the extraordinary game of chess."

With this explanation, Tuesday returns his focus to the game. Several people walk outside from the building and bum cigarettes. Lots of people smoke here, but very few people have cigarettes themselves. Then I remind myself, most of us wouldn't be here if we weren't in a state of desperation.

I stand and look through the open door inside the building. There is a couch and several chairs all oriented in the direction of a television set. Several people are watching a rerun of a show on the Space Channel. Oddly, there is someone sitting directly in front of the television with his arms outstretched to hug the box. Every part of his exposed flesh is inked with the most grotesque drawings. From the back of his neck, a gargoyle's hand reaches up over his head and drags its claws to leave blood streaked gouges across his shaved scalp.

By hugging the television set, I thought he was trying to hog it for himself, but watching for a minute I realize he is actually trying to make out with one of the characters on the screen. It is a disturbing sight. As the character appears in a dialog, he stretches out his tongue in an attempt to lick the character's face on the static glass. The frame of the picture alternates to a man with whom the lady is talking in the show and each time the man appears, the guy recoils with an expression of disgust. Then, when the lady appears again, he bends forward, amorously swooning and lavishing his affections while slopping his drooling lips across the picture.

Some of the people sitting around the television begin to comment, "OK lover boy, can we watch the show now?" Then eventually the voices become more demanding with frustration, "Come on! Get out of the way. We're trying to watch the show." Not only does the guy seem to lack any consideration toward the others in the room, he does not seem to recognize they exist. He is as oblivious to their presence as the images on the screen are oblivious to him.

Someone walks up and pulls the plug on the television. The screen collapses to a pin of light that quickly fades. The guy pauses, perplexed and puzzled. Now, the only image on the screen is the reflection of the room, far duller and distant than the excited and illuminated shapes that had bedazzled from the set before. Apparently his eyes adjust to see this reflection and his focus extends to notice the others sitting behind him sternly staring in his direction. He slowly turns his head as the orbs of his eyes oddly fix in strange, glazed spaces, then he stands and storms from the room.

The others sit at their seats silently waiting. Someone finally asks, "Is he gone?" Another person rises from their seat, peeks out the doorway. "Yea." He says as he flops back on the couch, then adds "When we finally start working, I sure hope they don't put a knife in that guy's hand." The television plug is reinserted in the socket, the screen flickers back to life and everyone's eyes return to the flashing lights that enchant their minds.

8

I return to the carport outside. Tuesday is gone. As others talk, I listen out for anyone mentioning news about work. People continue to arrive and move into the dormitory, but there's no work and I feel we're backing up against a wall. With my luck I'll be stuck up here with even more debt from the rent of the bunk and the meal ticket I purchased in advance of my first check.

Outside, I find my same seat on the concrete curb. Although this particular space looks like any other portion of the curb, for some reason it has a sense of familiarity to me, as if I am hoping that it has retained the warmth from when I sat before. As I sit I find it is stone cold again. It does offer an advantageous view of the chess game and it will warm with time; it will warm with me.

There are numerous conversations swirling around me. I can't really distinguish who is talking. I don't know anyone. Then from the chess game I hear the commentary arise,

"Lee? What kind of name is that?"

"What do you mean?"

"I thought you were supposed to be an Eskimo."

"Oh, give me a break. Am I supposed to be wearing a fur parka too and mush a dog sled to the grocery store to spear fish in the cooler, before sledding back to my igloo? You can't be serious?"

"But don't you honor your heritage, your tradition."

"First of all, I am not an Eskimo. I don't even know what an Eskimo is. I am an Inuit. We go by what we call ourselves, not by what others call us. You don't go by a name other people call you, do you? Of course not, otherwise you'd have 'schmuck' on your driver license.

"Second, I certainly do honor the traditions of my culture. In my opinion, the greatest honor I can give my ancestors is by demonstrating that I can be a man of my own time, that the fortitude of my people can survive in any climate, ecology or economy. And what more, I do."

The other guy rubs his chin either contemplating the game, his gaffe in the conversation or both

While waiting for his opponent to move, Lee continues, "And once I'm finished with another fishing season, I will resume my identity as a New Yorker. I'm already missing Manhattan."

I jump in to comment, "You live in Manhattan?"

"Yea, for most of the year."

"Yea, Geronimo traded in his bow and arrows for a camera and is a professional photographer." the other guy adds while his hand indecisively hovers over the few remaining pieces he has on the board.

"Whatever you say, pendejo." Lee razzes back, apparently their comments are in good spirits.

"Pendejo my ass." The guy responds still searching for a move.

"Have you moved yet? How hard can it be? You barely have any pieces left." Lee further baits his opponent and then turns back to me and says, "Yea, I've lived in Manhattan the last ten years. I come back to work some summers and see family."

"I was thinking of moving there." I add.

"Well, it's an extraordinary place. The way I see it, people go to Rome, or visit the Acropolis, or the Ziggurats of Mesopotamia, and wonder what it would have been like when those places were the thriving pinnacles of civilization gazing out over the expanse of human possibilities. In Manhattan I see it happening; I see it in the present. From there, I don't have to gaze into the past in search of grandeur, it is there before me and I am a part of it.

"Just think, every single culture of our species lives on that island, and we're not simply an idle presence, we all make our own contribution to what that place is, and we all do that by every one of us being who we are."

"You said you're Inuit right?" I ask.

"Yea,"

"What is Nunatak?"

"A nunatak is a rock outcropping on the tundra. It serves as a landmark and on the tundra, it is often the only land you see. The rest of the time you're walking on water, frozen water that is. Why the settlers named this town Nunatak is beyond me. This isn't Inuit territory. The Tlinget tribes live in this area." Lee's competitor touches one of his pieces and Lee gibes with a warning, "Are you sure that's what you want to do?"

The other guy pauses, hesitant, and withdraws his hand, then Lee adds. "I'm just kidding. You make your own move. Don't let me tell you how to play your game."

This statement seems to embolden the guy's confidence and he picks up the piece and moves it across the board.

"Finally" Lee declares, then quickly makes his move and adds, "Checkmate."

The guy lets out a grunt of frustration and Lee asks if he wants to play again or if he's had enough. The guy looks around and probably notices the rain then accepts the challenge. The plastic pieces clack as they are gathered. They set up to play, different sides of the same pieces in reflective positions until the first move is made and the game is sprung. The game becomes an alternation of hands reaching over the board, guided by their thoughts as they further entwine their lives.

9

I spot Tuesday walking nearby. He has a curious gait. He always walks with his head down. I can see his lips moving as if he is thinking out loud. Occasionally his head lifts to look around, like a turtle rising to the surface of a lake for a breath of air, before dipping back into the pool of his thoughts. He doesn't cringe in the rain. I wonder if he even notices that it is raining. He strolls back to the car port, steps under the cover and then sneezes.

I stand and approach him to ask, "Hey, Tuesday. Want to get a cup of coffee? It's on me."

He shrugs, and says, "Sure". I guess I'm making some sort of a friend. Poor guy. He seems somewhat lost, but really, he knows more about this place than I do. I doubt anyone else will befriend him; he has one of those quirky, eccentric personalities that others are more amused by mocking than understanding. Of course, my tendency to associate with outcastes often leads to my own exile, but I'm a big guy, I can do what I want. I find my strength in not needing to rely upon other's approval. I follow my own judgment and from talking with Tuesday on several occasions, I've found the guy rather fascinating.

We stroll into town along Main Street, although it should probably be called "Only Street", since it is the only one that is paved. I consider how the place resembles an old fishing village and then I realize that the place is a fishing village. The strait between the surrounding islands is too shallow for cruise ships, so there is little tourism. Of course this dampers the economy slightly, but it also gives an air of authenticity too, as if stepping back in time to when Alaska was a distant frontier of folklore. I envision images of burly men with grizzly beards matted with ice. I can see them trudging through blizzards over mountain passes. Some look back to see entire mountain sides of ice slide in avalanches that raze entire forests, snapping the massive trees like dry twigs.

Just then a brand new pick-up truck with shiny wheels drives by filled with local kids blasting the latest music. The image of a rugged setting with a sweeping vista is instantly transformed into the strip at Las Vegas. I can almost hear the kid's parents scolding disapproval of the boisterous music, similar to what their parents did when they were young and blared records of Ray Charles, Elvis Presley and Chuck Berry.

Tuesday leads us to a local coffee shop and we sit at a table, cradling the steaming mugs in our hands, sipping and savoring the warmth, as much, if not more than the flavor of the drinks.

I consult Tuesday for more information about work like when we will start, how many hours we will work, how much money I can expect to earn. I am here to work. I have bills to pay and debts to settle. I am not here to sit around and wait. So if we can't work yet, then let's talk about it, and hopefully with promising prospects.

"Don't worry. There'll be plenty of work soon enough, probably more work than you were expecting. Enjoy some of the leisure time before it begins, because once it starts, the work is relentless until the Salmon season is over."

"But there is nothing to do here."

"There's a trail where you can hike to top of the mountain."

"Really?"

"Yea, there's always a trail to the highest peaks of a place. People are always compelled to climb to get an overview of the lay of the land and there are as many tops as there are containers. Look at any place and you can discern the agreement of people's interests where their paths overlap. As for the trail up the mountain, I don't recommend it right now though."

"Why not?"

"The bears. They've been hibernating all winter and they haven't had a full meal for over six months. They're famished. For the time being, I'm staying out of the woods. When the salmon are running it's not a problem. They'll be gorging themselves at the river. But by then, we'll be busy working too."

"But what else is there to do around her except drink?" I sound a little theatrically exasperated.

"The activities this place offers are probably much different from what you're accustomed. This place is in the wilderness. There are boundless outdoor activities. Like anywhere though, you have to recognize the resources that are available and make the most of them. But keep in mind, the greatest resource you have is your own ingenuity."

"Yea, but what do you have to work with here? All I've seen is rain and wasted time." I say, resorting to a little friendly sarcasm.

"Well, the wasted time is your own fault. As for the rain, I always tell people that if it bothers you so much, why don't you move to the desert?"

"Ok, wise guy, then why are bars the only places to go in this town?"

"For a community this size, sometimes the only social establishments that can be supported are churches and bars. You have the watering holes for the spirit and water holes of spirits. People are social. We like spending time in the company of others. It is the most reassuring and immediate ways we feel part of something larger than ourselves. Look at us right now. We're paying a nominal fee for a refreshment to help support this tiny café that accommodates our leisure interaction. If you're looking for movie theaters, concert halls, museums and university lectures, you have to visit bigger cities. This community was made to fish. The big cities will still have about the same number of churches and bars per capita, but they have the abundance and diversified of means to support more. It takes millions of people to support something like Carnegie Hall, whereas here, the population can only feasibly put a few classical music albums on the shelf at the store.

"Every place has about the same proportion of people who share similar interest, but what I find fascinating is how certain communities inspire the populations to promote specific interests and the reasoning behind this. Cleveland is a great example. Cleveland has what is arguably the greatest symphonic orchestra in the country. Assembling a world class and historic orchestra is no easy task. You are assembling what is unquestionably the most intricate and complicated musical instrument that involves some of the most diverse arrangements of people, talent, emotion, repertoire, equipment, administrations, facilities and it takes more than just money. You have to have the right people in the right places and everyone making the right decisions from a variety of different angles so that all the variables correspond and coalesce into a singular accomplishment of exceptional merit, and not only do this once, but do this consistently. Then you need a community to appreciate and support it. It is a concerted effort of astronomical proportions. The city of Cleveland gets a lot of attention from around the world for that symphony too, and when I say the city, I mean the entire community."

"It's odd listening to you always talk about the sociability of people when one of the first things you told me is that you are always alone. Remember that?"

"Well that is how it appears, but I find it easiest to interact with people through books and music. Really none of us are alone. We all stand upon the accomplishments of our predecessors. We all live in the reliance of one another. Casual interactions are more emotional though. I'm too abstract. Conversations are concerts that we orchestrate around each other's interests and the best performances are when the interests orchestrated are of one other. When I talk though, I just vomit geometries. I guess I've learned to be content by simply trying to draw a perfect circle in the sand."

I pause for a moment to consider this and then add, "Well, your circles may not be perfect, but I think they're pretty neat."

After we finish the coffee we leisurely stroll back through town. Tuesday wanders off. I walk to the cafeteria to find that I missed lunch. I head to the break room again and buy a bag of chips to hold me over until dinner. While I'm groping through the crinkly bag and munching the fried potatoes, a lady walks by talking on her cell phone. I am not sure what astonishes me more, that there is cell phone service or the sight of a woman. The only women I've seen here are married.

Nunatak

She speaks volubly, "It's OK. I'll be back in a couple of months and we'll have some cash to work with. It'll be fine, don't worry. I've got a couple of months of hard work ahead of me, but it will be alright. Everything's fine. Sometimes we have to make sacrifices to get where we want to be. If it wasn't difficult, it wouldn't be worth it anyway. Everything's great now though. Yes, it's rainy, but it's still beautiful. The rain brings this place to life." She continues along a string of optimistic reassurance as she turns the corner.

Someone sits beside me on the curb and nudges me lightly with his elbow. "That's Carol. You know who she's talking to?"

I shrug. How should I know?

He continues, "No one. Her phone doesn't even work. She just walks around talking as if there is someone on the other line."

"Really?"

"Really."

"How do you know?" I ask, warily. I don't know who the lady is speaking to, how does he? He probably just heard this from someone else like he's telling it to me now. Honestly, I find her optimism comforting. I don't know who she's talking to. How could I? I hardly know anyone here, let alone whose ear might be open at the end of someone else's line. What I do know is that we're all in the same boat. We may have different roles, but we're all in the same boat.

He doesn't answer. He just shrugs and walks away. It seems I have already realized the most familiar expression here — the shrug. I shrug. He shrugs. She shrugs. They shrug. We shrug. It seems to be the only way to address this situation that one may never completely understand and that one may only hope to have the strength to accept.

10

Later in the afternoon I meet a young couple, Ross and Lynn. They're engaged. Of course meeting them only reminds me of Connie. She said she would come with me. Having never done this before, I didn't know what to expect except that people said it was harsh and miserable work. I couldn't subject her to this.

The couple is adorable. I can see how they lean on one another, how they have committed themselves to face the world together. That is what I want. That is what Connie wants too. Why don't I want it with her? I want it to last a lifetime. I want it to last forever. I want it to be held with the indissoluble bond of love. Why can't I feel that? Am I capable of feeling it? Am I capable of any other sense in the world except the pain I subject myself to?

I am able to make dinner that night. Of course when I say that, I mean make it on time to eat and not miss the meal. The only cookbooks I know are menus. However, I can make a great pizza. I make it with a telephone. Instead of pulling it out of the oven, I pull it out of the front door. Just listen for the chime and it's ready.

Garrett Buhl Robinson

11

In the morning I check what is commonly referred to as "The Board." On the administrative building, there is a miniature "A" frame roof extending from the outside wall that shelters a cabinet where a list of the names of all the employees is posted. I suspect the tiny roof is built more from necessity due to the perpetual rainfall rather than attempting to resemble the niches for icons ornately built into the sides of Cathedrals, but "The Board" is revered all the same. There is always a mob of people crowded around it every morning checking for work.

The assignments are indicated with a system of highlights. This morning I can see that very few names on the list have assignments. Those few who are lucky enough to work, are highlighted in blue. I check the legend to see that this indicates working in "Cold Storage", although I haven't the faintest idea what that means. I thought the people who weren't working are the ones being kept on ice. For everyone else without a highlight, there is a note with the handwritten message: "Check Back Tomorrow."

At breakfast, I bump into Tuesday. After we finish eating, we stroll through town for our regular coffee and chat.

I ask him what he plans to do with the money he earns this summer.

"Principally, season tickets to the Cleveland symphony." He says.

I couldn't be more surprised, but I suppose from talking with him, I shouldn't be surprised by anything. "No kidding. You were talking about symphonies yesterday, I should have figured. Are you a big fan of music?"

"I'm interested in all the ways we communicate. Music is certainly one of the most intriguing."

"Do you play any instruments?"

"The only instruments I play are the radio and records. I have taught myself how to read music though which provides more insight into the performances. It's not as involved as playing an instrument, but it does allow me to engage my attention more."

"Do you like any popular music?"

"I like all types of music."

"What about Rock and Roll?"

"Sure."

"What about hip hop?"

"Sure."

"No way, you like hip hop?" I would have never expected this.

"Yea. I'm not sure if you're familiar with the structures of ancient Greek drama, but many rap songs follow similar measures with the Prologue, then Episodes with choral strophes and antistrophes, that make various turns in the development until reaching the close. It is a classic formula for delivery and quite effective."

"What about rock and roll."

"Well rock and roll, like jazz, is an offshoot of the blues. Mainstream rock and roll songs generally follow one of the most basic structures of the blues, whereas jazz branched off into phenomenally inventive and improvisational directions. Blues itself developed from old spiritual hymns. If you've ever heard hymns in church you would certainly recognize the basic formula of revolving stanzas and repeated choruses along with the common themes of lamenting tribulations and sacrificial redemption. They are expressions of consoling as much as congregating. Personally though, I am more interested in music without lyrics."

"I like the lyrics. They tell me what the artist means." I say.

"And that's your preference. For me, lyrics diminish music's expressiveness. Lyrics often reduce the music to a mere ornamentation of the words and words have limitations. Some of the most powerful moments in life are beyond description and there is no surprise that we often find ourselves at 'at a loss of words' in intense moments. In those instances, just because we cannot say something doesn't make it any less real, or mean that it doesn't exist. There are more languages than those composed with words. Math is a language. Horticulture is a language. If you consider language as a means through which we interact with one another and our environment, then life itself is a language."

"Yea, but doesn't language mean tongue, like 'lengua' in Spanish?"

"That's right, so it would seem to refer to the act of expression, but we shape words with more than our tongue. Also, listening is as important of a part of speech as speaking itself. So, why don't we say we speak one another's 'ear' instead of speaking one another's 'tongue'? Words can be remarkably distinguishing, but they can also be diminishing. Words are simply arbitrary references; labels we use to evoke a sense of reality in which we may relate together. The languages of which I speak address a broader range of communication and some languages are more suitable and effective for particular situations.

"A kiss is a far more effective way to express affection than simply to say 'I love you.' The statement can be nothing more than a ruse, but to actually trust someone enough to close our eyes and render ourselves most vulnerable and touch where we are most tender, is one of the most convincing ways to express the sincerity of our affections. Not only does it show our affections. It is our affections. After all, love is more than a declaration, love is an offering."

Tuesday seems to sense my discomfort with the directions of the conversation. Perhaps he thinks I am misinterpreting his statements with innuendo, but really, my discomfort is in how they evoke my memories of Connie.

Unflustered, Tuesday continues, "Music is a language too. Music is arrangements of pitches and tones sequenced in rhythms. Yet it can be one of the most, if not *the* most, emotionally evocative means of expression we have besides some of the most impressionable physical interaction like a kiss or a punch. Yet, despite its evocativeness, it is abstract. Instead of using a symbolic system of reference such as words to share our feelings, music accomplishes this without reference. It may be the one medium of communication which most closely resembles our processes of thought.

"I am not sure if you have ever climbed to a mountain peak, but I have and when I did, I felt a similar sensation of rapture that is evoked within me by the symphonies of Beethoven. If you play an allegro movement from a Beethoven symphony to anyone, they will get excited. If you play Beethoven to whales, they will get excited. Every person is moved with the compelling rhythms of tribal drums. Every person is alerted with the sharp clarion of brassy winds.

"Or startled by a truck horn that sounds like a charging elephant." I scramble to make some contribution to demonstrate I am following his explanations.

"Yea, that is a great example. Now, imagine developing the means to arrange frequencies of sound that could stimulate the taste of ice cream, without the ice cream, and not just the taste but the texture and temperature. After all, our experience of events, such as eating ice cream, is simply how it is experienced in our minds.

"This doesn't mean we can use music to explain Quantum Physics yet, but of course Quantum Physics is a system of symbolic representation. We don't live in symbols. We live in sensation. And not only is music the most profound way of sharing the sense of life, it can create a path upon which people may synchronize their lives. It is more than a rhythm; it is a shared experience. There is no mystery in why music plays such a prominent role in religious ceremonies and sports events. Music can simultaneously be an individual catalyst and a collective adhesive."

"Well this certainly adds a few more dimensions to the phrase 'getting into a groove.'"

"Yea, and keep in mind although that phrase is musically related, it refers is to the playing of LP records. It is another example of the material basis from which those referrals originate and upon which we relate. What has interested me lately is our growing acceptance of increasing complexities of musical arrangements. Musical arrangements that would have been considered dissonant five hundred years ago, sound quit mellifluous and harmonic now. Even pieces by Mozart that dairy cows find soothing and relaxing were often considered infuriatingly complex centuries ago.

"In the upcoming season of the Cleveland orchestra, there are a number of polyphonic and polyrhythmic compositions. In a very simplistic way, they are like pendulums of different clocks swinging as they fall in and out of rhythm with one another. One can hear them slowly converging until they synchronize for a single swing and then slowly diverge again, in the alternating ticks and tocks of their distinct tempos. But instead of doing this with the metronome pendulums of clocks, imagine the correspondence of complex melodic phrases with different chords, different rhythms and tempos interacting in the most boggling way. Each phrase cycles through its own pattern so one must listen beyond the brevity of the particular to recognize a broader correspondence of them all. The novel developments expand the expression's harmonic correspondence with our biological being. After all, there are far more ways of agreement than monotony.

"I believe this is an invaluable lesson for contemporary society as our species becomes increasingly integrated into a more directly interactive whole. There has always been the necessity for conformity in the past, and reasonably so. Our lives overlap upon the avenues and systems through which we interact. We must have standards through which we may utilize these systems together, like traffic laws. However the means by which we interact are diversifying and multiplying at rates that are unprecedented. There are still nationally broadcast networks, but now our systems of interaction are elaborating in ways where every single person can have their own channel and even multiple channels through which they can announce their individual interests, insights and ingenuity into the world. The general populace is becoming less of an attendant audience and more of an elaborating performance.

"In the past, unity was sought and secured in homogeny, but the strongest unities are collectively corresponding diversities. Our lives will radiate like streams from the sun, extending in every direction and it is no surprise that music is one of the foremost means of exposing the population to this reality. After all, music has been utilized by our species to instill a sense of social continuance since our ancestors danced and chanted their myths around bonfires with the rhythm of their coordinated participation.

"Of course the notion of broadening an audience's perception of reality is nothing new in the art world. That is one of the things artists do: make associations in the unexpected. Some artistic movements have been based entirely upon the notion of breaking down preconceptions to render the audience more open for the unexpected. Think of Dadaism or the Theater of the Absurd. Think of Cubism disassembling visual reality and reconstructing it in from multiple perspectives simultaneously. It can be employed with the directness of Wilde's *A Portrait of Dorian Grey* or with the subtlety of starting a performance late to offset an audience's timing from the inflexible expectations of punctuality. Removing oneself from the ruts we find entrenched in life is a common ordeal. We need the reliance of regularity at times, but we can also overlook opportunities along the well-worn paths of the marching masses. That is why people tend to see fewer opportunities in life as they grow older. It is not because they are less capable, but rather because they will not allow themselves to see the present by only looking through the past."

Here, Tuesday suddenly stops, picks up his cup and seems to recede in his seat into some distant tranquility of quiet contemplation. It is like a tumultuous ocean suddenly shrunk into a placid pond. Perhaps he is recharging his batteries, I don't know. I am tempted to look and see if he is plugged in somewhere.

"Well," I feel compelled to say something, "I guess that sums up a lot, now doesn't it." Really, I feel a little dizzy. Buy a stranger a cup of coffee sometime and you might be surprised. After a minute or so I can't resist asking, "Tuesday, where did you go to school?"

"I went to the library. Nothing against schools, they are the most important institutions we have, but we have the greatest repository of information in human history and it is completely open to the public. I simply went to the library and read through the shelves like I was eating corn on the cob. I still do."

"Do you have any specific interest?"

"Yea, everything."

Garrett Buhl Robinson

12

That night there is a commotion in the dorm room. While I quietly read in my bunk, I hear some guys explain how someone got drunk and freaked out. Apparently the guy tried entering the wrong room. When people kept pushing him out, he went berserk. He pulled a knife and began swinging the blade through the pinch of the door as he tried slashing through his stupor.

"He's passed out now, so leave him alone." Then the same voice continues, pleading for an explanation, "Why did y'all let him drink so much and then leave him in the bar?"

From this, I am comforted to know that our local Jack the Ripper is one of my roommates. I pull open the curtain to fix some faces with these voices.

Then someone enters the room with an air of authority. He holds a pen knife in his hand and asks, "Is he in here? The police are on the way."

"Awe, come on man. You called the police?"

"The guy pulled a knife and started swinging it in the air. You're damn right I called the police."

"It's a pen knife, not a machete. What are they going to charge him with, attempt to make a paper cut?"

"He could have taken someone's eye out with this."

"Come on. He's drunk. He passed out. It's over."

"No. It will be over when he's out of here."

"But he won't even remember this in the morning."

"Well, I doubt he ever forgets waking up in jail."

I pity the guy. I almost feel like arguing his case. Most everyone has had a humiliating experience with alcohol. It can take your mind and release a beast.

There's a pounding at the door. A police officer enters. "Where is he?"

His friend hesitates at first, but then relents and leads the officer back to the bunk. I can't see around the corner and I have no motivation to walk over and gawk. I'm relieved that there is no commotion, just a few moans from an awkward and dazed rousting. Shortly afterwards, the officer props our cuffed and staggering marauder out of the room.

I lie back in bed and draw the curtain closed. Tonight's show is over.

13

The next morning, I don't allow myself to sleep late. Compelled with a sense of diligence or perhaps desperation, I rise early. I have removed the snooze button, if not from my travel clock, at least from the options of my own discretion. If I want to sleep late, then I should set the clock later. It is time for me to determine what needs to be done and do it. I don't have time to flip flop and flounder. I have work to do. I have a job to perform. I have money to make and bills to pay. I have my earnest responsibility to demonstrate, if for no one else, than at least for myself. I am ready to begin etching my renewed life on a clean slate. I jump into my jeans and untangle my shirt over my torso as I run to The Board. And what do I find to greet my noble resolve and dedication: disappointment. No work today, not for me a least. I suppose even the greatest intentions are often snubbed by stubborn reality. Here it seems the standard routine.

I slump to the cafeteria for breakfast. I feel like a broken egg sizzling on the griddle, but I don't even get that sunny side up, what I get is a single serving of yellow scramble. Filling my tray, I see the couple, Ross and Lynn, whom I met the other day. They offer a seat at their table before I can ask. It's nice to be remembered. They tell me they're visiting the beach today and extend an invitation to me.

"Sure." I look for Tuesday hoping he might be wandering around. After the meal, I search for him outside. I tell Ross and Lynn to go ahead and I'll catch up. It couldn't be too hard to find them, after all there is only one road and one continuous coast on the island. Tuesday is nowhere to be found and I finally give up and jog to catch up with the couple. The asphalt of the road crumbles into gravel until it is pulverized into dirt where muddy puddles have accumulated in the grooves dredged with spinning and slinging 4x4's. Ripples pulse on the puddles from the tinkling of otherwise invisible drops of rain.

I reach the couple before they veer off the road onto a small path that winds like a cave through the thick vegetation. I feel like I'm tumbling through the most luscious wonders. The tips of leaves tipple tiny sips of water on my hands as they part a path through a living curtain that undulates into the thickening forest. I remember past visits to deserts where the plants are thick skinned and spiked, stinging stingily like scorpions with the scarcity. Here the ground bursts with supple ferns fanning in every tickling breeze while the trees outstretch and overflow with mossy limbs. The bark of the pines is sticky with syrupy sap. Birds flutter between berry speckled bushes. The ground softly gives with each step like a lavishly layered matt. The air is rich in exhaustless oxygen.

Lapping through the forest, the sound of the surf rhythmically builds in my ears. Clambering and scampering over a few glossy boulders, I am greeted with the unexpected.

Nunatak

When I think of a beach, the image that comes to mind is sand and the sun. Here there are only stones, a cobble of clumsy rocks garbling down to the water. There is no silky sift of silica that warmly slips softly between one's toes; there is a riddle of knobby obstacles tumbling like rubble into the icy sea.

From this, I lift my eyes into the most glorious sight I have ever seen as Bald Eagles fill the air. There must be fifty of them swarming, whirling in their own course, gliding and swooping to the surface of the water where they extend and outstretch their talons to grab some morsel from the sea, then swing the meal to their beaks while their broad, powerful wings swish gusting strokes that ponderously lift them as they swim upward through the thinning ocean of atmosphere until their circling, riding glides plume back to the soaring sky. Some alight upon the whorl of their woven nests, tearing pieces of meat between their clutching feet and hooked beaks to dangle the nurturing morsels above the stretching, extending reach of their chicks hungering to fledge and molt and grow to rising heights. Others perch upon the tops of the trees that tip and bend with their weight while they lift their open throats and sing.

Along the road and down the trail, the paths guided the three of us in a line. Now, in the open I veer away from the enamored couple who cling to one another. They seem to guide one another around, showing each other every interesting discovery. They obviously and completely share their worlds. I think of lines that sound like something from Rainer Maria Rilke's poems, "Tell us lovers what tender wonders you touch as you reach into the world through one another."

"Hey, check this out." They shout at me.

I walk over to where they are standing and they point out some drawings on the rocks.

"These petroglyphs are about 2000 years old. You would expect symbols of fish and food. But look, most of them are geometrical figures."

"It makes you wonder what they were thinking." I comment.

Lynn shouts, "Check this out."

Through all of stones, there are a number of large rocks that they point out. I can see that the rocks are aligned in particular ways that suggest they were set in place with some intention.

"These are fish traps. See how they funnel into a narrow point. When the tide went out they set basket at the base to catch the fish. These fish traps are as old as the petroglyphs. Perhaps the geometrical figures they etched on the rocks represented something they thought to be gathering their thoughts as they were gathering the fish. I know they always entrance me every time I visit here, either in person or in my memories."

I begin searching over the rocks looking for more petroglyphs. My wandering steps eventually lead me to the edge of the water. I pause for a moment and open my focus from the individual stones to take in the panorama. Across the channel the continental mountains rise into jagged, snowcapped peaks. The steep slopes line in rows of ridges of solid stone that ripple across the continent, eventually crumbling into the grassy, Mid-western plains wrinkled with waterways.

My mind wanders as my thoughts float through the images of the petroglyphs as the petroglyphs float through my thoughts. These mysterious messages span centuries as they were passed directly from the hands of mystical figures, etched with the interests of their minds and now speaking directly to me as they provide a continuous thread through which, in some way, I am able to gain a sense of those ancient times. I wonder if they ever considered that those messages might be read across a span of countless seasons changing through generations along an unfathomable length of linked lives. I wonder whether what they said was intended to speak to me or anyone else, or only to speak of themselves. All that I do know, perhaps all that I can, is that some of what they express is a sense of their wonder that I feel in my own way now.

Suddenly I look down and notice that the rocks are covered with shells of tiny clams. I take a step and hear them crushing beneath my feet. As I walk directly away from the shore, it sounds like I am trudging through the crunch of snow. There is no powdery fluff around my footsteps though.

The sound is from me destroying those tiny creatures' homes, those tiny creatures' lives. They secrete those shells from their own being, for their own protection, but beneath my devastating steps they are crushed. I look back at the sea and think how easy it would be to drift away into the deep, to glide upon the waves as the liquid would lift me from my feet and hold me aloft in a buoyant embrace. Then I consider the icy needles of cold piercing through my skin, wedging and cleaving me to pieces as I crumble and dissolve between the picking fish, till my bones clatter over the stones, tumbling with each tossing wave. As I ponder this image, gulls and crows descend into my footsteps. They begin ripping the clams from the shattered shells. They shriek and screech in the raucous gobbling glut of a frenzied feast.

"What's wrong?" Lynn must notice the melted expression on my face.

"I feel like everywhere I go, I only leave a path of destruction."

They look back at the gathering of gulls and crows bickering and tearing the shreds of meat between the stabs of each other's rapacious beaks. Ross looks back at me, somewhat sympathetic, somewhat incredulous, then says, "Well, you haven't seen nothing yet. I heard we start work tomorrow. You do realize that we will be working in a slaughter house? What you see here will be magnified a thousand times."

14

The next morning when I check the board, the list of names is lit up like a rainbow. Every name is highlighted, even mine. The Blue highlights are for Cold Storage, the Pink are for the egg room, Yellow are for the Can Line and Green are for the Fish House. My name is marked with the optimistic shade of green.

Walking out of the locker room, my rented rain gear still has the creases from the folds in the wrapper. I look and feel clean and new in my gear. I clop down the planks of the deck in my galoshes. I adjust the gloves, tugging to extend my fingers to the very tips. With the exception of my face, my whole body is wrapped in rubber. I feel like a bouncy new tire in yellow rain slicks as bright as a lemon.

I ask my way around and finally find the fish house. Some guy wearing grey overalls dappled with smudges of grease and oil opens the door and gracefully waves me inside. There is a pan on the floor with a brown liquid. Someone in blue coveralls instructs me to step in the pan and dip my gloves in a bucket with a similar liquid. I notice the magic marker lettering that spells out "Sanitizer". He shouts, "This is people's food. This is your food."

I walk into a large room where people are already working. The space is partitioned with monstrous machines that rage in a chaos of clacking and smashing commotion. Plugs are stuffed in my ears to protect my hearing so the sound is muted, as if I am underwater, but the noise still seeps through and pounds relentlessly. I look down and notice I am standing in a pool of blood. The red velvet swirls with dirty water and I lightly lift my feet to pat the puddle in disbelief. The space is dim, not necessarily from lack of lighting, but rather because it is thick with moisture, blood, as if even the air is bleeding. Everything looks like it's bleeding. The machines drip with blood and ooze with offal as they occasionally spit out fish heads while chewing their grisly meal. The fish heads on the floor stare into space from their lidless eyes as their mouths gape in a detached gasp.

Everyone seems to know where to go and what to do. I spin and twirl in circles as I am caught in a swirling drain of blood and guts that surrounds me. I try to attach my attention to anything, searching for some slot to fill, some function to perform, some contribution to make, but everything blurs with the splattering gore and I feel myself helplessly flailing, falling on my feet, sinking where I stand.

A tap on my shoulder saves me from my melodramatic maelstrom. I turn to see someone in raingear who shouts over the machines. "What are you doing?"

"I don't know. I just got here."

"Well first of all, if you're assigned to the fish house, you need to be here at 7:30, OK."

It's 8 o'clock.

"Grab a squeegee." He points to one leaning against the wall by the door. "See these drains?" He points to a backed up pool of blood with a pile of intestines clogged in the center. "Unblock those drains and squeegee the blood and guts and fish heads to clear the floor." He then drags me over to a circular table where people are standing. They pull carcasses of fish from the table's center and neatly and efficiently hack their sides with knives before dropping them down some shoots. "See that blocked drain?" He points down a crawl space beneath the table. "Take care of that. All the guts, fish heads and blood go down the drain." I am glad to hear that I am not included in that list of mauled pieces committed to disposal. He then pulls the hood of my rain coat over my head. "You'll thank me for that. Now get to work." He adds before walking away.

I crawl beneath the table to clear the drain. I can feel the dull thuds of chunks of fish dropping on me. I approach the fish heads which seem to be frozen with an expression of ghastly terror. I scoop them into the drain and the pool quickly shrinks. I watch the stream of crimson fluid pour down the dark hole. As the stream tapers to a trickle, there is a loud sucking sound from deep inside as if the pipe is already craving for more.

I inch back from underneath the table, finding an open space I can crawl out, then pick up my squeegee. I quickly stoop to glance under the table to admire my first accomplished task, but I can see that more fish heads have already fallen and the drain is backing up again. I crawl back through a puddle of blood while clumps of guts, fish heads and dismembered fins drop on top of me and then splash and splatter on the concrete. The machines scream, the whole place bleeds and everyone keeps working. This is one hell of a way to make a living, crawling through a pool of bloody sludge that drains, drops and plops in gobs from the lacerations of slashing, gnashing death. This is mayhem. This is a slaughterhouse floor.

In time I work my way through the room. Through this, I begin distinguishing different areas by their signature mess. In the back of the room at the top of the line, there are huge brine reservoirs. These reservoirs of filled with fish. As they are needed, individual gates open and the fish are sluiced down the lines. This sends a cold, limp, flipping, slithering slimy river of fish flesh oozing down a shoot where a conveyer belt lifts them onto a machine's table. From this table, workers rapidly hook each individual carcass on a spinning, chinking metal tread that quickly and incrementally files them into another section where a slamming, hammering sound corresponds with each entry. This is the sound of the machine lopping off the heads and slashing away the fins, then gashing the belly and eviscerating each body. With the speed the machine runs, the carcasses do not properly align every time as they pass through the inner workings. This results in the partially gnawed and chewed fish heads spitting and spewing onto the floor. As I work around these machines, I begin to distinguish the sound each makes as it performs its specific function. This cacophony of machinery is accompanied with a chorus of polyglot hollers as the workers yell over the clattering and roaring of processing.

To touch up any missed fins or any pieces of the head that are still attached to the body, the carcasses are spun onto the circular tables. Here the workers pick up the individual fish, neatly trim away the inedible excess and then send the meat on their continued way toward the inside of a can. The green that highlighted my name seems to be less a sign of optimism and more of a smear of the slime line of the fish house.

Garrett Buhl Robinson

15

By law, from every 2 hours of work, there must be a 15 minute break. Before walking out of the Fish House for my first break, I see a line has formed at a hose. Everyone takes the time to wash the blood off their raingear. For the most part, each person can accomplish this themself, but no one can rinse their own back. So as need generates innovation, mutual need generates cooperation. Each person alternates with the next, rinsing each other before leaving. After rinsing, I follow the crowd which leads me to the break room. There is hot coffee, tea and cookies for everyone and I take care not to allow my sleeve to drip on the food and drink. I can only hope others have shown the same consideration. I'll find out soon enough when I eat because I've never heard of sushi flavored cookies and hopefully that is not what I'm having for break today.

When I find a seat, I ask the guy next to me some questions. He tells me that the people in the blue jump suits are quality assurance and they make sure everything is done within the health code and the company's own standards. The people in the grey overalls are the mechanics. He explains that some of the canning machines were built in the 1920's. The technology apparently has not changed much. They replace parts from time to time and constantly adjust and tighten the bolts to keep them running, but as long as the metal housing of the machines don't rust, they will practically last forever. The blend of conversations maintains itself as a ruff grumble with an occasional hoot or holler leaping above the steady droll. Then someone flickers the lights and everyone shuffles back to their place in the line.

Returning to the fish house, I walk to grab the squeegee, but a supervisor taps me on the shoulder. "Ever cleaned fish before?"

I shake my head.

"Let me show you."

He guides me over to one of the cleaning tables. The knives have no points but are rounded at the end of their length. I suppose there is no need for any stabbings at the place. The knives are also tied to the tables with heavy duty fishing line. A red light begins to flash which corresponds to the sound of a loud buzzer as the de-heading machine lurches into motion and hammers away. Soon, the gashed carcasses begin piling up in front of me. The supervisor grabs a fish and holds it in the palm of his left hand.

"You see these fins? Cut them off." He then demonstrates how this is done, deftly removing the pieces from the fish as his hand nimbly moves the blade. He flips the fish in his hand to inspect the other side. "See, OK." His approval indicates that the other side of the fish is fine as all the fins had been removed by the machine. He then drops the fish down a shoot that carries it to a conveyer belt that transports it to another segment of the line.

He then grabs and scrutinizes another fish and efficiently makes the specific cuts, then another and another, in a building rhythmic sequence of grab, slash, flip, slash, drop, with an improvisational chop and hack occasionally thrown in for good measure. As each fish flops down the shoot, another is grabbed. Now, instead of just demonstrating what to do, he demonstrates how quickly it must be done. "You gotta work fast so the fish don't pile up, but make sure you're thorough. No fins in the cans." He pats me on the back and I take this as my signal to go.

The operation is fairly easy. I feel I have mastered it after a few fish and begin moving through the motion as unconsciously as walking. Instead of sauntering through a soothing setting though, this is a treadmill of slimy skin. The novelty is quickly lost and the work becomes a drudge of monotony.

At this point, considering my private tutorial in the art of cleaning fish, plus the number of fish I've already cleaned while mastering the technique for myself, I know I must have covered a considerable amount of time. I look up at the clock and to my surprise, only 5 minutes have passed since the last break.

To pass the time, I count the number of seconds I spend cleaning each fish. I begin comparing my performance from one fish to the next, attempting to identify trends and isolate performance peaks to make adjustments and maximize productivity. I formulate a veritable spread sheet in my mind and I begin marking the fields with an imaginary rubber finger dipped in slimy blood. The whole time the dead flabby flesh of each fish flops in my hand, slime oozes down my slicks, the knife flashes and pieces are cut away. After this elaborate and extensive measurement of my performance, followed with a statistical evaluation, I look up at the clock again. Ten minutes have passed since break.

Crunching numbers with statistics begins to sound like the cartilage in my hand so I redirect my thoughts. I allow my mind to drift and I am pleased to find it retreat into sweet places of serenity. I begin elaborating. I concentrate on specifics. I envision soothing settings of absolute tranquility. I find myself soaring over an image of the Himalayan Mountains. I can see their soft robes of snow draping over the lofty peaks of cloud grey granite and then watch as the mountains turn into farms of rice patties that step down the surrounding hills in ringing tiers. I ascend the steep slopes on the Islands of Hawaii and pass above the glow of bubbling, molten rock. I watch whales joyfully leap from the lagoons and crash back into the water with laughing splashes. I can see the elegant fanning of their flukes and the nimble lengths of their flippers as they gracefully glide and sing through the deep. I watch the Wright Brothers set sail into the sky with a bumptious motor whirling the blurring circle of a propeller and see the skids leave the ground and watch those glorious wings bank over the dunes as the path of mankind rises into the sky. I see the foamy waves splashing against the rocky shores along the coast of Maine as a striped tower lifts a beacon of light. I follow the winding line of the Mississippi and broadly fan across a continent with trillions of tributaries. I bend my neck to gaze steeply into the crowns of towering Redwoods. I circumambulate volcanoes in the cascades. I climb steep temple steps on the Yucatan Peninsula and gaze out over the surrounding jungle. I see the sun set upon the pyramids from across the Nile. I watch blue icebergs float by a sailboat that cuts through the stormy seas along the coast of Antarctica. I visit Easter Island and set the palm of my hand on the coarse chin of one of the mysterious monolithic faces where Polynesian ships must have turned from the shores in terror convinced of an island of giants before continuing to the coast of South America and their trace dissolving into the continent to arise upon the Andes with the Incas. I look and listen for Darwin's finches on the Galapagos while watching the lizards diving into the ocean and count the slumberous steps of tortoises that have lived for centuries. I stand beneath the Eiffel Tower and look up through the lattice of engineering climbing above the city of light and then watch crowds set their watches as Big Ben gongs at the House of Parliament along the slow flow of the Thames. I gaze at St. Basil in absolute astonishment at the elaborate magnificence accomplished with bricks. I leap from one fantastic sight to the next as I spin the globe of the earth beneath my steps of dreamy thought. Then I look up at the clock and twenty minutes have passed since break. Time seems to have practically stopped.

16

Eventually the clock does creep around to noon tick by excruciating tick. The supervisor walks around holding up his index finger. Then yells, "1 o'clock people. Everybody back at 1 o'clock." Another supervisor shouts, "1 en punto."

I rinse with everyone else and return to the locker room. The lockers are really made out of chicken wire with wooden doors mounted on small swiveling hinges and a latch where we attach the combination locks we rent. With the moisture, the chicken wire allows ventilation. The place is soaked. Outside it rains. Inside, where we work, is a slosh of all types of fluids splattering from the depths of the ocean to the sweat on our brows. Beneath my gear though, I am pleased to find that my clothes are dry with the exception of a little perspiration. I don't mind this. At least it is my own fluid and not from the fish. I smell my hands and either they don't smell like fish yet, or I'm already desensitized to the scent.

Arriving at the cafeteria I can see why people were rushing out of the locker room. The long length of the line for food twists and winds into the curved figure of an eight in the sign of infinity. I guess I'm in for a long wait. I jump into an available space of the millipede wait. I am immersed in the swirling currents of the surrounding conversations. The sound seems oddly muffled though until I realize that I haven't taken out my earplugs. As I do, a sudden hiss rushes into my head like the pop of a bubble of equalizing pressure in an airplane's gentle slope of descent.

I hear someone behind me complaining lightheartedly, "This place is just one long line. We work in a line, we wait in a line, we eat in a line, and our bunks are set in a line so we even sleep in a line."

Someone responds, "Life's a long line, a line that begins and ends in oblivion. All that matters is how you weave yourself with others in the patterns of the tapestry we compose together."

"Sure thing Socrates."

Another says, "I'm glad the fish are finally here."

Someone else enthusiastically agrees and yells, "Yea, the salmon are here. All hail the fish." Suddenly several people begin to repeat "Fish, Fish, Fish." The place erupts into the accumulating chant while people begin banging the tables in time. I hear "pescadro" shouted along with the others, blending the mono- and the polysyllabic with an interesting musical quality. The chant continues as if the unanimous chorus will summon more fish, calling them to rise from the deep.

The uproar slowly begins to fade as everyone's interest returns to their plates and the mouths that were bellowing before, become quiet as they chew their fill of food. As the sound of the school of fish evoked by the crowd tapers, someone shouts, "Shut-Up! In a month you'll all be sick of fish."

Nunatak

Someone grumbles, "What a sour-puss."

Then someone else, "Sour-puss, are you serious? What the hell is that?"

Another banter begins building as occasional phrases incite mind after mind as excited commotions rise and ebb like the tides. Compared to the limbo of the previous two weeks, everyone is enlivened with the engagement of work.

I spend half the break standing and waiting for the meal. By the time I'm served, the line is gone and the wait is over for everyone.

While I eat, I hear more languages than I can count. I can recognize some Spanish in addition to some other European languages, but there are a number others that I haven't the vaguest idea of what tongue is spoken. The anatomy is the same but the movement is different. In many of the conversations, I'm sure people are discussing situations I could immediately relate. They are probably describing experiences we had all shared only moments before, but their descriptions are made in ways that are as distant to me as the moon. From some threads, familiar words are spoken like "Cold Storage" or "Cannery" in the statements of different languages. I wonder how the Inuit I met the other day while he was playing chess feels when he hears the name of this town spoken in the phrases of so many languages, like a familiar figure briefly breaking the surface of the indistinguishable seas of other's distant speech, a quick flashing point upon which different lives suddenly coincide.

Then the lights in the cafeteria flicker and someone shouts, "work", and another "trevajo" and then again in one language after another as everyone rises from the tables and pours out the door.

17

Through the remainder of the day, my hand grows increasingly sore, but I simply work through the discomfort, even when the discomfort turns into pain. Eventually calluses will form and my muscles and joints will adjust to the strain.

Despite the excruciating monotony of the work, I continue exercising my ingenuity by developing ways to distract myself from glancing at the clock. I'd never thought of a time piece as an addiction, but suddenly I've found the clock to be the greatest temptation I've ever encountered. The clock's looming face stares heavily upon me with the feeling of the inevitable. I turn away but there is simply another clock on another wall. As I try to avoid them, they seem to multiply, replicating themselves in every direction I avert my gaze. I close my eyes and the hands click relentlessly in the darkness. Even the surrounding machinery begins to sound like the inner workings of a clock that I am trapped within as the circular table turns into a gear and every fish a cog I grab as I am twisted like a winding key. If I let myself go, my mind might unravel like a watch spring in anticipation of the next fix of a break, that short escape teasing me to relent and surrender into hopeless abandon, and dispatch my life into dejected despair along with the heads and fins of the fish I cut to pieces.

I look at the clock, the one act tragedy I just performed in the theater of my skull, which is hardly the

Globe, had a brief five minute improvisational performance, and with only one ticket sold, I doubt it will make it to Broadway. The most I can expect is a five week run in Alaska before it's canned. It's more vaudeville anyway as I comically juggle a knife and a fish upon the Wheel of Misfortune spinning on this circular table before me.

While I work, I notice my knife is different from the one I handled before lunch. The design is the same, but the face of the blade narrower. My grandfather was a butcher and from seeing his old knives, I know their blades wear away over time. The blade I held this morning was fuller, like a gibbous moon. This one has been slowly etching away like a waning crescent. The older blade may not have the same strength, but I'm not using it to pry. In a competent hand they both work well. Both their edges sharpen the same.

I work until dinner. After dinner I work into the night. The last fish runs through the line around 10 PM. Everyone is released in the fish house and as the last fish works its way through the rest of the canning line, each person leaves their station as if a string was pulled from a necklace and each individual bead bounces off in their own direction.

In the locker room I hear someone say that there will probably not be any work tomorrow. The local boats will be out fishing the next couple of days and we'll have to wait for their return. I find myself hoping this is true. I am not already tired of work, but it will be nice to have a day's break so my hand can mend. This brief, initial strain allows my body to know what to expect. I should be able to adjust through a quick recovery in a day's break. Then I'll be ready to work through the whole season because I hear once it's fully underway, it goes on relentlessly for well over a month. Then once it's over there's nothing until next year. I can consider myself lucky to have suffered the misfortune at the beginning. Better to learn early than lose the entire season.

Before turning in to sleep I walk to the bathroom to brush my teeth. I bump into Tuesday. He is standing in front of the mirror flossing. As he pulls the floss from between his teeth, he turns his head to the side to avoid splattering food particles onto the glass.

"Now there is a man I can respect. Even in the most dismal circumstance, working at the most dejecting job imaginable, you still have enough self-esteem to make extra effort in maintaining yourself by flossing your teeth."

He looks at me and says, "There have been many times in my life when all I have had is my dignity. If I have nothing else, I will always have that."

When I make it to my bunk, I don't anticipate any trouble falling asleep. Working from 8 AM until 10 PM is an exhausting stretch. I will see how I feel when the work day is even longer and there are no days off.

Garrett Buhl Robinson

18

The next morning I arise early to check the board. As I approach, I begin to suspect what I might find. People crowd around the posting. Fingers point up at the board and then slowly lower to track their eyes down the long list. Each jerks to a stop at their own place like alarmed hands of a clock and I hear blurted expletives, euphemisms or otherwise, all expressing the emotions evoked by their frustration in starting the day without an assignment.

I arrive at the frayed edge of the crowd and begin climbing in as others are squeezing their way out. Trying to keep my feet amidst the jostling mob, I see that there are a few names that are highlighted, but with most of the others, I find my name is not. Looks like I have the day off.

As I struggle to crawl out of the crowd, I hear someone shout, "Yes! Listen to you all, 'wah, wah, wah,' crying like helpless little babies. I'm working today."

I hear someone ask where and he tells them cold storage. He sounds like he won the lottery. I consider approaching and congratulating him, but from the sound of his revelry, I wouldn't say he needs any affirmation. But I also take into consideration that his winning ticket gives him a pass to clean fish. But judging from the disgruntled crowd, it is the object of interest held in the highest value, and he has it. Really, I suspect that his excitement is not as much from the assignment, but the recognition from the supervisors that the quality of his work is of rare value, or perhaps they just recognized his name.

I bump into Tuesday and I ask him if he'd join me for another cup of coffee. While we're walking down the street, there is a ladder propped up against the side of one of the buildings. I notice that Tuesday carefully looks overhead, but then walks underneath the ladder with little concern.

"Well, I can see you're not superstitious."

Tuesday flinches with a little surprise at the sound of my comment. He seems to be startled whenever anyone expresses interest in him. "Oh no, not in the sense most people would describe it." I can tell right away that I am in for a lengthy explanation. The most common and banal topics seem to unfold in the most expansive ways through his consideration. "I can't say that I have found an explanation for every superstition, neither would I claim any of my explanations to be conclusive. My reasoning is not always rational. But as I always say: logic is an extremely important and effective tool, however one must not limit oneself to it.

"As for walking underneath a ladder, there seems to be a very practical purpose in the superstitious belief. If a ladder is propped up against the side of a building, there is a high probability that some type of work is being conducted above and thus, there is a high probability that something could be dropped on a person walking below. For that matter, someone could say that it's unlucky to stand underneath roosting pigeons or that it's unlucky to jump out of a flying airplane without a parachute. It is simply a matter of the probability of misfortune befalling upon one. But instead of dismissing the superstition or thoughtlessly following it, there is a need to search for the meaning behind it. There are plenty of people who would have reluctance about walking underneath a harmless ladder, but wouldn't think twice about walking underneath scaffolding being disassembled over a sidewalk, or a piano being installed through a window in an overhead apartment."

"Well what about a lucky rabbit's foot?" I goad further although I am not sure if I am more interested in finding an explanation or simply trying to stump him.

"I haven't given a rabbit's foot too much consideration, but obviously it is a type of charm. Perhaps people wanted to keep some affinity with the animal, so they would keep a part of it with them. In the past rabbits weren't just cute; they were a meal for a family; they were a prize for sustenance and survival. Or perhaps it is a desire to gain some attribute of the rabbit such as its swiftness or elusiveness. Perhaps it was a toy given to children so that no part of the animal would be wasted and these toys could have been cherished and retained as sentimental reminders of past parents."

"What about the bad luck in breaking a mirror?"

"I would speculate that is based upon the value of mirrors in the past. In a common household even one hundred years ago, there was often only one mirror and it could be quite small due to their expense. The taboo on breaking them could have served as a deterrent from handling them carelessly and save an unnecessary expense for replacement. Also, in the past, mirrors were used almost exclusively for viewing oneself. Breaking a mirror could be considered an act of self-destruction and such a disposition could be worse than a curse.

"Like I said though, this is purely speculation and I'm just prattling off whatever explanation I can quickly deduce and describe."

No more superstitions come to mind with which I can try to stump him. I am not sure if any of his explanations are correct, and of course he makes no claim that they are, but he offers something in response beyond perfunctory obedience or reactionary rejection, he offers consideration which I find quite refreshing.

While we walk, Tuesday continues to talk. The flow of his expressions passes smoothly through our arrival and entrance into the café, transforming from one topic to the next without the slightest pause even as we place our orders at the counter and take our seats at the table.

Finally, he decides to pause long enough to take his first sip from his mug. I use the opportunity to state the obvious, "Tuesday, you seem to have an elaborate opinion about everything."

"Well, it's funny you should say that because 'everything' considered as an all-inclusive identity is really interesting. If "everything" is entirely all-inclusive, then it must include "no-thing". Perhaps this could be considered as little more than a linguistic paradox, however it has some profound implications. It implies that an essential component of what something is, is what it is not...."

Then off we go again. From here, he launches into an explanation of how arrangements more massive than clusters of galaxies, even more massive than our entire universe, can be assembled from the contents of a vacuum.

I mean, "the contents of a vacuum", what?!

I decide to change the topic and consult his opinion on something a bit more familiar to me, "Tell me then, what's your opinion of some political issues, say about the conflicts in the Middle East?"

"Well, first, there are far more human conflicts than just in the Middle East. In my opinion, we are too concerned with whose winning the fights, when we should really be concerned with why we are still fighting each other.

"But to answer your specific question, I simply say that all the sons and daughters of Abraham should remember that they are brothers and sisters. Was God not upset when Cain killed Abel? Anyone who teaches that brother should kill brother or sister should kill sister must be mistaken. People should live in peaceful activity and prosper."

"What about the Persians, then. They're not direct descendants of Abraham?"

"We are all brothers and sisters."

"That is a very simple answer."
"Yes, and it is true. We all share a common source."
Well, I can't really argue with that.

19

Later in the day, I wandered around with a buzz from my morning conversation with Tuesday. Really, it is hard to call our talks conversations. It is more like me sitting and listening to him as my mind races to keep up.

In ways, he reminds me of a few actors I have known. It didn't matter whether they were in costume or not, they were always performing. They would probably even try to sleep in the most convincing way possible. Their lives were devoted to the projection of personality and the enlivenment of entertainment, and the cost of admission for their improvisations was often simply attention. Every setting was their stage and anyone's interest was applause. They could accentuate any atmosphere and elevate any interaction into the profoundly sublime simply with their talent and enthusiasm. I would simply sit back and enjoy the show of their lives.

With Tuesday, it is a little different. His shy voice draws the attentive ear closer so that a person finds themselves peering through the lens of the eye of his mind that magnifies and telescopes each ordinary day into a revelation. Perhaps his life is like a laboratory for mixing carefully measured ingredients into extravagant reactions. Perhaps his life is a chalkboard for sketching elaborate theories and just peeking inside his halls fills any interest with lengthy lectures. Perhaps his life is like a library where he walks around pulling dusty books from shelves to open brilliant pages with passages that lead to any place imaginable.

Some might think these encounters as transient events, flashes of insights that vanish as suddenly as they had appeared. As I walked alone this afternoon, I thought differently. Retracing the conversation, reconstructing the information and revolving the different shapes of ideas Tuesday conveyed, I wonder to what extent I may be adjusting the patterns of my thought to his influence. Certainly I have to adjust to anyone to understand them from their perspective, but I began to wonder if my mind is like a glass of water that moves in the ways it is stirred, that pours into the shape of the situation it fills and often overflows.

After all, our minds are the supplest portions of our body. To gain a tangible understanding, they can contort into any shape they encounter, they can stretch between stars and galaxies in celestial calculations, they can narrow to atom slice precise, broaden to span aeons of time, and they can shape themselves into their own creations they can imagine. Comparatively, the body's extremities are the clumsy parts.

Then, continuing through my mulling stroll today I witnessed two remarkable events. At one point I watched a raven behaving in the most ingenious way. The ravens here are different than any I have encountered before. They are much larger than typical crows. There are crows here too, but the ravens are well over twice their size. This afternoon

96

while I walked along the shore near the cannery, I saw a raven flying with a stone in its beak. It dropped the stone from a height of about fifteen feet in the air. At first, I was astonished at the stupid futility of picking up a rock, laboriously lifting it into the air, only to drop it back to the ground. Perhaps it had the notion of building a stone castle instead of a nest, but lost interest as it realized the burden of effort required of this ambition.

After dropping the stone though, it then immediately swooped down and began pecking at it. It then picked it up in its beak and lifted it into the air from where it dropped the stone again. This time, finding the rock among all the others strewn across the beach, the raven pecked at it until I saw that it pulled the meat of a clam from its shell. I am still wondering how the raven was able to figure that out. Perhaps it was when someone threw a rock at it sometime before. Poor birds, they certainly know what it is like to be hated simply for what they are.

Eventually I wandered back to the work site. I needed to visit the stock room and pick up more earplugs. Obviously I need earplugs for work, but I've also found I need them in the dorm. People seem to congregate in the room and talk and this is quite a distraction for me while I read. After all, the people are saying something intended to be heard and listened too, and although it may not be specifically directed to me, it is simply my nature to try understanding what they have to say. Some people can read through any type of commotion, but conversations or any type of parlando sounds can be quite a distraction for me.

Of course, contributing to the commotion with my complaints seldom brings peace. In fact, it typically aggravates the situation by embroiling the others. The easiest solution is simply to plug my ears. Who knows, from what I'm reading, sometime in the future I may be able to make a contribution to their conversation. Then, in regards to my interests, their conversation could be transformed from a disruption into an affirmation. For the time being though, I accept the divergence and without letting it pull me apart, I simply develop my life within the space it provides as they are otherwise occupied.

After visiting the stock room, I walked out on the planks of the dock to see if any boats were unloading. Peering over the edge, I noticed a few seals swimming below and I paused to watch. The wildlife at this place is supposed to be legendary, but I've heard the most dangerous animals are released after our first check and found in the bars, thrashing through the shattered glass of emptied containers of alcohol. What I have seen in a sober mind is far more interesting.

Of the swimming seals, there was one which caught my attention by behaving peculiarly. Instead of diving beneath the surface as the others do, that is plunging forward, leading with the nose and arching its back to dive, this one would do a type of backflip, diving in a completely opposite way. It almost appeared the seal was playing a game, improvising its behavior for the pure pleasure of a dynamic difference, perhaps attempting to set itself apart for attention and potential admiration, a social strategy that often spoils by only raising suspicion and contempt.

I lingered for a while watching as the whiskered faces of the sleek seals returned to the surface, releasing a mist of held breath before replacing it with the refreshment of another, then diving back into the enveloping sea swarming with the fleeing fish they chase in fluid grace. While I watched, I noticed this one seal kept diving opposite of all the others, persisting in its back flips and I became convinced it was more than a game. There must be some reason besides sheer joy. Animals behave through necessity. After all, I am not spending this summer in a cannery for the sumptuous pleasure found through the experiences of working in a slaughterhouse. The promise of joy or happiness is simply another psychological enticement, another appetite our minds have developed to sustain our engagement in the wages and trades of life. I too am hoping to obtain some benefit whether it provides an exit or an entrance, if there is any difference.

Again, I question my motives for this summer's excursion. After the fishing season, I should have a few thousand dollars to work with. What will I do? I wonder how a seal feels when it sinks its teeth into the soft flesh of a fish. Does it revel in the accomplishment of the catch, is it satisfied with its fulfillment or does it think how this one meal empowers it to reach another in a life fraying and fretting as a line of endless hunger?

Lying in my bunk, reading, I look up behind me at my clock. It is time for dinner. I swing my legs out to sit at the edge of the bed and begin tying my shoes. As I stare at my fingers knotting my laces, I notice something. I notice my nose. It is a big obstruction for my vision and I realize what may have been the motivation for the seal I observed earlier. The seal must have realized that by diving backwards it improves its vision. When the other seals dive forward, plunging in their hunt, much of their range of vision is obstructed by their noses. When the other seal dives backwards, it will be looking up into an unobstructed field of vision. After all, it is not hunting for its nose, it is hunting for fish; it is hunting for something beyond itself.

Leaving the building, my feet thrumming down the flights of stairs, I think of what Connie may be doing right now. Every time I visited her on Saturday night, I always found her in the same place, sitting in front of her easel, lifting a brush in her nimble fingers, dabbing the bristles with paint and then vividly stroking the canvas to life with the elegant figures of her mind drawn into existence with her touch and attention. And what have I been doing? I have been hacking my way through the bounty of the sea like some barbarian, like some ravenous savage.

20

Tonight, there is no line in the cafeteria. With most everyone off from work today, the crowd has scattered. Setting my tray of food on a table, I take a seat by myself. There are others around, in fact a number of groups sit at surrounding tables, but the closer the proximity I have to strangers, the more severe my sense of isolation.

I lift my eyes from fidgeting with my fork in my food and notice Ross and Lynn walking by. I burst the sullen bubble I was building and signal for them to join me. I noticed during our visit to the beach, that I thoroughly enjoy their company. As individual's they are interesting, but as a couple they are much more. They truly live their lives together. It is not as if they get mushy and start feeding each other in the cafeteria, but their lives appear to be emotionally attached in a way that seems they could never be apart, that there is always some portion of one within the other, that their lives were intrinsically linked in ways that could overcome any sort of separation.

Lee walks by and I invite him to join us. I announce him as the chess master of the island, a title he modestly dismisses. Introducing him to Ross and Lynn, they begin conducting the informal introductions of one another and seem well on their way of making their own acquaintance. Noticing them off and involved with one another, I look up to see Tuesday weaving his way through the seats between the tables. He sees me and there is a slight sense of a shutter in his step, as if he had instinctively lurched to turn away but tried to refrain himself knowing I had spotted him. One might think that he was shirking from the debt he owes me. I doubt this though. That doesn't bother me. We haven't gotten our first check yet. I would say it is the group that bothers him more. He probably thinks that he would have to surrender himself to join, and for such a solitary person, surrendering himself would be to give up all he has. I know exactly how to handle this very delicate psychological issue though, "Tuesday! How are you doing my friend. Come on and join us." By making it absolutely clear that he is accepted just as he is.

He responds to this kindly, warmed with the welcome. The faint hint of a smile even rises on his face, which he tries to suppress and not give himself away, just like those subtle smiles sometimes seen on people walking alone as if they are savoring some sweet secret of a cherished memory in the worlds within worlds revolving in the musical spheres of society. Of course, what is actually happening in his head is something I can only make the wildest guess. I can ask him what he thinks, but I have learned that this generally leads to a full-fledged dissertation.

Ross, Lynn and Lee seem to have strolled off on a conversation together, refreshed with the scenery of each topic they introduce along their overlapping paths. I ask Tuesday a question but his only response is a demurring nod.

From my interactions with him over the last week or two, I have noticed he only has two modes of discourse, either an inundating outpouring or staunch silence. At a table with unfamiliar people, he seems more inclined toward the latter as he quietly dissects his meal.

Having composed myself with what I have found to be familiar, gathering the few contacts I have made, I become detached as my attention drifts into the surrounding sounds. I hear someone at the table behind me ask, "Hey, what time is it? Hey, you've got a watch don't you? What time is it? Oh never mind I can see it. Hey, did you know your watch is upside down? Why do you do that?"

There is a pause and then I hear someone else explain, "I'm not concerned too much about the numbers. They don't mean anything to me. I am more interested in what the watch says. Have you ever noticed how the upside down numerals on a digital clock resemble letters? Well they spell out words. Through the day I'll have these unexpected urges to look at my watch and when I do, I see what the letters tell me about my life."

"Well it's 5:06 right now. What does that mean?"

"Goes."

"What, ghost? What are you talking about? How does 5:06 mean 'ghost?'"

"Not ghost. 'Goes'. When you see it upside down and read it backwards, 6 is a 'g', the 0 is an 'o' and the 5 is an 's'. That spells 'g-o-s.' You add the silent 'e' in conventional spelling and it spells out 'g-o-e-s', 'goes'. It is a favorable sign of progress, that I am moving forward in my life."

"That's has to be the single most absurd thing I have ever heard in my life." The guy sounds very convincing in this declaration too, then he continues, "You can't be serious in thinking that has any meaning."

"Well what meaning do the numbers on the clock have?"

"They're the measurement of time. It is a means by which we can coordinate our lives. We established a standard upon which we all agree, and upon those increments, we synchronize our schedules. Now what time is it? Oh, 5:07? What does that spell? The '7''s an 'L', the '0''s an 'o', the '5''s an 's'. That spells 'l-o-s', then 'you add the silent 'e' in conventional spelling'" here the guy add a satirical tone from quoting the exact phrases the other guy had made before, and continues, "what does that spell, 'lose'. Is that a favorable sign? I'd say it's more like you lost the argument."

"No, now it says 5:08, like 'Bozo'." The guy with the upside down watch retorts, "The '8''s a 'B', the '0''s an 'o' and the '5''s a 'z'. Then add another zero at the end to fully reflect your character and you spell out 'Bozo.' Oh wait. No, now its 5:09, that makes it 'bozo' again, but with a lower case 'b'. Perhaps before you may have been considered a more formal 'Bozo', now your just a trivial 'bozo'".

"So you're telling me that every single minute has some meaning to you that's spelled out on your watch?"

"No, every single minute has lots of different meanings. My life is rich with meaning and sometimes, yes, it is spelled out on my watch."

"You're crazy." Seems to be the other's final say on the matter.

"5:09 could also be 'boss' or 'sob', or perhaps even S.O.B.." Someone else adds. Apparently the issue has stirred interest in several people, myself included. This is a bit outrageous. Who would imagine an argument developing over this?

"You see." The guy with the watch adds, "How can you say I'm reading something into nothing. Now you are all seeing words on my watch. Stop it. Get your own watches. Try reading an analog clock."

"No, an analog clock just keeps asking 'Y'." Yet another guy pipes in, his obnoxious laughter indicating that he is extremely amused with his own comment, or perhaps his laughter at his own joke is an attempt to convince everyone else it's funny. "Get it, the letter 'Y' for the question 'Why?' The three hands of the clock? Oh come on, you guys don't see that?"

"This has got to be the most absurd thing I've ever heard." The guy who originally asked the time says. "You all are just making this up as you go along. As Nostradamus here was describing, 5:09 would be 'b-o-s', or probably more realistically, just a bunch of 'b.s.'. If you're going to change it around constantly why don't you spell out '9', and take the 'n-i-n' for 'nin' and then add the 'e' at the end and you have 'ninny'. Then 5:09 becomes 'so ninny', which I would say perfectly describes this whole issue. That's what time it is. So synchronize your watch with that. I'm just trying to figure out when I need to make a phone call and you all are trying to decipher encrypted messages from a delusionary world. You can do what you want I suppose, but I'd like to try coordinating my life with reality. OK?"

"You know you can drive yourself crazy trying to interpret every tick of the clock that way." Now, yet another person joins into this lively discussion. A lot of people seem to have a number of opinions on what most everyone seems to dismiss as being completely absurd, "I know this guy who has a compulsion for reading license plates on cars. But he's always depressed and all he ever sees are depressing messages. He will see 'LSH' and he will think of the scourge of a 'lash', but I ask him why he doesn't see the enjoyment of 'lush'. He will see 'DES' and immediate think 'desperate,' or 'dead' but then I ask him why he doesn't see the abbreviation for 'destiny', or 'desirable' or 'deserve'. He is simply using some generalization of the world to confirm his predetermined opinions. Most of the time, we don't see reality as it is, we see what we believe. Reading those messages doesn't provide any insights. It's only a source of distortion. There is no question that everything in existence has significance, but that doesn't mean everything in existence has personal relevance to him."

It certainly sounds like an interesting conversation, but then I wonder why I am sitting at a table surrounded by people I know, in fact people I invited to join me, and then my attention immediately turns elsewhere. Perhaps this is my problem. I am never satisfied with what I have.

Just then I hear Ross say to Lynn, "Did you hear that? I just heard someone at the other table say more fish are coming in. Sounds like we're going back to work tomorrow."

21

The next day I have a new assignment. Instead of my name being highlighted in green, which I suppose is fitting for the slime line at the Fish House, it is highlighted in blue for Cold Storage. Looks like I get to find out what the guy was so excited about yesterday.

After suiting up in my gear, I ask around and finally find the facility on the opposite side of the complex. Just as the cannery, the work site stands on the stilts of the long dock. A fork lift whizzes past me. Its wheels rapidly clack over the planks as if they are a xylophone's wooden bars that all play the same dull note.

The inside of Cold Storage is far more open than the cannery. In fact, it looks like a huge warehouse space. Along one wall beside the entrance, there is a swarm of large rolling racks. Judging from the icy mist rising from these racks and the frost crystalized over their skeletal frames, I suspect they were rolled from the freezer and I will assume these freezers are what put the "cold" in the "storage". People slide large trays made of shiny stainless steel from the racks' shelves and then loudly drop each tray upon a table. Really, dropping isn't the proper description. Rather they slam the trays on the table as if trying to exercise some hostility from their lives. As each tray crashes on the table, the stiff bodies of the frozen fish awaken and rigidly flip through the air as they are broken away from their icy adhesion. Released from the trays, the fish are swept onto an adjoining table where they are set in boxes. They are packed two at a time like shoes in a box, or yin's and yang's fixed chasing each other's frosty tails as they cycle, or rather, are peddled out of the ocean and into commercial trade.

From the far side of the warehouse, I see more racks emerge. They barge through a passage that apparently leads from the freezer. The threshold into the artificial artic is covered with long, broad strips of plastic to serve as a buffer for the air flow, while still not impeding the passageway. The racks are pushed by Samoans dressed in insulated jump suits. The palms of their thick mittens are crusted with ice from handling the rolling racks. I'm not sure how many hundreds of pounds of fish each rack must carry, but they twirl them around with ease and park them in the crowd with the others.

About thirty yards away I notice someone waving at me who is apparently a supervisor. The supervisors all wear the pants from the raingear, but not the jackets. I suppose they expect the occasional splatter, but without having to reach into the fishy lines, they don't need the coats or gloves. Of course, they wouldn't be supervisors here if they hadn't spent plenty of time on the line themselves. The tools of their trade have become the workers they supervise, just as the conductor's instrument is not the baton, the conductor's instrument is the orchestra.

There is a long, large behemoth assembled from conveyers and tubes, racks and trays in the center of the warehouse.   People are lined up on either side of the assembly as if prepared to lift it together and carry it away. When I reach the supervisor, he says, "Come on, stop day dreaming or you'll get run over around here." He pulls me into a space in the middle of the line. There is a piece of metal attached to a long clear tube dangling from overhead. He grabs the piece of metal and places it in my hand. "You're spooning. Ever done this before?" The bewildered bulge of my eyes must answer his question, because he immediately continues. "Watch the others in front of you. When the fish come through, scoop the carcasses clean."

He backs away and tidies up the line, tapping a few people on the shoulder and pointing out something in their oversight. I lean forward and look up the long stretch of people in which I was inserted. A forklift approaches and parks at the top. The engine revs as it lifts a large blue tote. The totes are basically big square buckets that hold about 5000 gallons of fish. The supervisor waves his hand over his head to signal the start. A siren light flashes as the machines lurch into gear. The conveyer belt wheels in front of me and I hear a suction sound awaken from the tube attached to the spoon in my hand.

The lifted tote tilts toward the tip of the line. Hundreds of fish pour over one another as people work in a frenzy to set each one individually on a machine that lops off their heads and eviscerates their bodies. Each fish is set on its back in a slot on the conveyer belt.   As the fish approach, I watch the others. With one hand they grab the flap of the slit belly and with the other hand, they slide the spoon through the carcass. When they do this, the clear plastic of the suction tube blushes with blood. When the fish arrive, I do the same.

As I work, I find myself counting again. Typically the only thought of counting I enjoy is that of a dancer's graceful steps through the fluid measures of music. But here there is no enjoyment; there is only endurance. Here counting is a way to track through the monotony, a way, if the only way, to say that everything is not the same.

My counts begin with the rate the fish are passing. I am cleaning about 1 fish each second, or 60 per minute and in the 105 minutes between each break, I am working through over 6000 fish in each segment of the day and if I work a full day from 8 AM until midnight, then I will work through 42,000 fish and they will be the exact same 42,000 fish that everyone else performed their assigned task upon as we are all strung along the same line. It is like trying to qualify my existence by the number of heart beats in my life. What do several billion cardio muscle contractions mean? Do I get a check for them too? Perhaps so, but a check for the heart won't be from a payroll department, but would be done by a doctor and that may not be a good sign.

I look at the clock but the only time it shows is eternity. Sometimes I look up at the other workers. On occasions are eyes meet and are fixed in a frozen moment. We may speak different languages, but we all have the same expression. We have all migrated and converged here from the furthest reaches of the planet as we chase the vast runs of salmon.

On some rare occasions the conveyer belt stops. When this happens, I feel my body begin to lean to the side. With my attention fixed on the motion of the belt for such long periods of time, when it stops, my body unconsciously compensates by leaning to the side and I have to catch myself before I topple over. I look at the stopped conveyer belt, but it appears to still move, slowly shifting and sliding to the side in a blur of my mind. It is like the odd sensation of walking on an escalator that is still. The mind tries to anticipate a momentum and the first steps float in a numbed sense of awkward uncertainty. It is an odd state as the mind tries to adjust between the expected and the actual.

The conveyer belt lunges back into motion and I resume spooning out the blood and viscera until break. I find this job is messier than working in the fish house. The spoon and the suction device often sputters globs of blood up from the carcass and inevitably this splatters onto me, often in my face. I learn very quickly to keep my mouth shut while I worked here, otherwise I would inadvertently end up drinking plenty of raw fish blood.

After break, they reposition me at the end of the line where there is a crowd of racks. After the fish are cleaned, they are weighed individually and then sorted into slots. From these slots, I pick the fish up two at time, one in each hand with my rubber thumbs in their mouths and my fingers hooked through their gills and neatly and tightly arrange them in rows on the trays in the racks like big sardines in a can. As a rack is filled, I roll it out of the way and replace it with an empty one. It is a little less monotonous than the other jobs. Plus, there is a sense of urgency as the fish stack up in the slots. Instead of simply standing in front of a conveyer belt as a fixed appendage of the machine, it is more of a game. I am still filling a need, but in more space to elaborate.

Loading the racks, I find there are five different types of Salmon we're working with. There are the King, or Chinook, salmon which are the largest and apparently fetch the best price at the market. Then there are the Sockeye which have the firmest, reddest flesh and are the most preferred by the Alaskans. The next in quality are the Coho whose meat isn't quite as firm and red as the Sockeye's, but still a stout fish. A fourth type are the Chum which are rather flabby. The pink salmon are reserved for the cans. Apparently they have the softest body and are the easiest for the machines to squeeze into the tiny compartments of tin packaging. Sometimes the Sockeye are canned, but for a very small market. For the most part, the better body of fish are sold whole and then cut into steaks to be grilled.

I learn the identities of the fish through hands-on instruction. The person at the weighing station would shout the identity of the fish before sliding it into a slot where I retrieved it. Soon, I am able to identify the fish by the organization of the slots where they were found. This leads me to learn how to recognize the fish by their own characteristics. It is an odd pedagogic system, but it works and I am slinging and sorting fish by the tons before I know it.

Garrett Buhl Robinson

22

At dinner, I ask Lee and the others about some details of Salmon fishing. I decide that instead of chasing the conversations that circulate around me, I should engage the people I know and with whom I may speak more directly.

Lee explains some of the details. Depending upon the type of salmon, the fish will stay out at sea for one to five years. They always return to the same river which they were spawned. They trace their way back by a sense of smell. The fishing boats do not use bait. They do not use sonar. As the schools approach the inlets the salmon grow excited and begin leaping from the sea. They can be spotted from the boats by the commotion they make on the surface of the water. The purse seine boats then approach the schools of fish and launch the dinghy. The main boat and the dinghy will take either end of the seine net and encircle the school of fish. When the boats meet at the completion of the circle, they cinch the bottom of the net and draw in the catch.

When the season is fully underway, to save themselves time and fuel, the fishing boats will sell their loads to relay boats that return the catches to shore. Then the seine boats can stay out on the water and fish.

Lee continues, "What I find most remarkable about the industry is that this is the last food resource for mass consumption that remains wild. Every other food source that is mass consumed, beef, pork, lamb, vegetable produce and anything else you can imagine is all domesticated. Granted there are a lot of fish farms these days and it is becoming more domesticated, but a vast portion of it remains wild."

"The fish farms are undercutting the prices and driving the fishermen out of business." Ross complains.

"Yea, but people are willing to pay more for wild salmon, just like people are willing to pay more for organic produce. I'm sure that both the farmers and the fishers will be able to stay in business." Lynn clarifies.

"Well, sooner or later, and probably more sooner than later, the population of the planet will surpass our means of food production, then what are we going to eat?" Ross says.

"Frosted Cake." to my surprise, Tuesday contributes a comment.

"Ewe." Lynn says, making a universal expression of disgust, obviously finding the option sickeningly sweet.

Tuesday recoils at the initial reaction and is surprised to find everyone's attention suddenly turned in his direction. Then, he noticeably recomposes himself, overcomes his reluctance and explains, "Well, it is a kind of joke. I guess you all didn't hear about that professor of nutrition who conducted the study where he only ate frosted cake. It was a national sensation for a while."

Everyone pauses in silence for a moment. "Yea, I heard about it." I say, surprised that no one else did, or is unwilling to admit it. "He claimed to have lost twenty pounds by eating nothing but cake for two month."

Tuesday continues. "What he was actually studying is the effectiveness of dietary supplements. Frosted cake provides starch in the breading and sugar in the frosting, but it provides scant vitamins and minerals of nutritional value. Ross is right. We do seem to be approaching a crisis in food supplies and there is the possibility that we may need to rely upon algae and synthetics to supplement our diets and that would require that we would need to supplement all our nutritional needs. We may not live off of frosted cake entirely, but we have to live off of something.

"If anything though, I thought the professor's marketing scheme was brilliant. After all, what other academic nutritional study have you heard about on national news? Too few, no doubt. But we hear about every single diet craze in the world."

"I heard one recently that claimed for a single payment of $19.95, a person was guaranteed to lose weight if they stopped eating." Lee adds.

Tuesday nods in appreciation that Lee is following his line of reasoning and then continues, "Falling in place right along with the trend, who wouldn't be interested in hearing that a person could lose weight by eating nothing but cake and have a college professor of nutritional studies at an accredited university make the claim."

"Yea, five out of six psychiatrists would say that is crazy." Lee parodies a common advertisement ploy.

Everyone has a laugh, then someone from a neighboring table interjects in the direction to Lee, "You're not Indian."

Lee is a bit astonished with the blunt interruption. Even he seems a bit blustered before responding, "Of course not, does it look like I come from India."

"I mean, you're not Native. Natives are supposed to be quiet and somberly wise. You talk too much and you're always joking around."

"Well, I apologize for my inconsistencies with your misconceptions of me. Maybe later we can discuss this in my teepee while we pass the peace pipe. Oh, if you're waiting for the 'somberly wise' part, how about this, 'Wise man say, few men recognize more intelligence than what little they possess themselves.' How's that?"

I decide to divert the direction of the conversation, and ask Lee, "Where is it you live in New York?"

Lee takes a moment to adjust again and calm his composure, then explains, "Well it's funny you should ask. I happen to live directly next to a very prominent high rise. In fact, my apartment has a completely unobstructed view of what I find to be an extremely distinguished portion of that building's brick wall. I hardly live inside though. I only sleep there. I live in the thick of the city and every time I step outside, I have arrived."

I tell everyone that Lee is a professional photographer in the city. Lynn asks, "What do you photograph?"

"Everything I find interesting. I must admit though, I do a lot of festivals for local papers and I have had to do quite a number of weddings too."

"You should come down to Long Beach and photograph our wedding." She says.

"I may just do that, but what I'm really interested in is photographing the buildings."

"Well, then you're in the right place if you live in Manhattan. Do you have any favorites?" Ross adds.

"There are so many I like, I can't even say which I like best. What I concentrate on is not the individual buildings though, I'm more interested in capturing their correspondence with one another. To me they actually speak with each other. They feel like ancient figures observantly standing as the traffic passes. I like watching how they turn through the light of the day and twinkle in the night, the windows of their eyes blinking and flashing with the life inside.

"There is a huge project that I have been working on for years now. I have been collecting panoramic photographs from each building I can gain access to the roof. It creates a type of puzzle, a puzzle which I am assembling the pieces and which elaborates as it continues. You can never see the building from where the photo is taken, but you can see all the surrounding buildings. The location of each shot can only be recognized as the viewer pieces together an image of the city from different perspectives."

We each finish our meal and there are a few minutes where we linger and lounge, but soon we return to the dock, slip back into our slicks and find our places in the processing lines.

After dinner, we work until 10 PM. When the forklift driver loads up the last tote of fish he honks the horn ecstatically. Everyone begins to cheer. It must be nice to be the messenger of good news. The rest of the time he simply does his job, his principle expression is the revving of the engine as he darts about, sliding the forks under tons of fish, lifting them up, rolling them around from one designated place to the next and then setting them down in a process of retrieval and delivery that keeps the operation flowing.

Regarding the last tote, 5000 gallons of fish are processed in a few minutes. Each time I turn to pick up two fish and before turning to sling them onto a rack, I peek down the length of the line. As the last fish rolls down the conveyer, the people are released one at a time to follow the course of their lives through their free time.

My station is the last to leave. Only the supervisors linger longer. The last fish is weighed and dropped in the slot. I set it on the tray and roll the partially filled racks to be labeled and pushed into the freezer.

I rinse and walk across the docks in my rain gear. My locker is still located by the Fish House on the other side of the facility. Until more pink salmon arrive, they're floating the personnel. Just like the hunger of any animal, we adjust to the need.

Several fishing boats are tied to the dock. There are huge vacuum tubes about two feet in diameter that are extended into the hulls to suck out the fish. I can see the unloading crew frantically working. Someone stands at the edge of the dock watching. I ask if there are any pink salmon. "Oh yea, lots of pink."

I suppose I'll be back in the fish house tomorrow.

Garrett Buhl Robinson

23

The next morning I check the board and find my name is highlighted in green. I put on my suit for work, rain suit that is, and slide back into the slime line. Working through the day, I can sense the irritability rising in people around me. I can sense it rise within myself. Sure, there is dissatisfaction in every instance of life, but this is more than that, this job is really disturbing. We are literally wading through death. I'll catch myself making a mistake, or someone else begins slacking and burdens everyone else down the line or a million other ways everyone can get on everyone else's nerves as our lives rub together in the abrasion of an intense situation. Emotions flare. Tempers erupt. We're all in a bad mood and we've all got knives in our hands. If this is a dream job, it is a nightmare.

There are many times people displace their frustrations on me. They're mad at something and they seek relief by taking it out on someone else. It's not personal, but it is negligent. Of course, there is always the temptation for me to take my frustrations out on others too. I resist this though. I refuse it. I am not going to perpetuate something I find disagreeable. I am not going to pass it on with the justification that it was passed onto me. I don't direct my life by the decisions of others.

We're all wallowing in the same offal from the same fish as we try cutting and hacking our way out of a desperate situation with what earnings we can garner. As bad as it is, it could be worse. After all, we could be the fish. They were just returning to their place of birth for one last exhilarating thrill. They were completing the cycle they were compelled to follow, urged to birth the strained clutch of eggs or to sow the swollen sacks of their seeds. They had traced the finest particles of their origin in the vast dilution of the ocean. Then while approaching the intensifying scent of sweet nostalgia pouring from the rivers of their birth, leaping in anticipation to climb the rushing waters of their origin, they hear the ominous sound of propellers chopping through the waters; they feel the nervous frenzy of confusion in the school swarming around them. Suddenly they're seized in the tightening knots of a net and lifted into the thinning gasps of the air and poured into a smothering hull of a boat, drowned in nothing more than their own likeness. They may be dressed again, but not in the flowing gown of the ocean, not in the elegant ruffles of the rivers, they will be dressed with garnish on shiny plates and lifted and examined on fine cutlery, or maybe they'll be dumped from the can and stirred with globs of mayonnaise before being spread across slices of bread. That's the raw deal as we all may, or may not, wonder what awaits us.

During a break, while I'm hunkered over my weariness in my seat, I hear Carol walk by. She is still talking on her cell phone, or is she just talking *to* her cell phone. Either way, I hear her, "Yes, the fish are coming in. We're finally getting to work. Yea, of course it's tough but it's what I've committed myself to do and I'm going to do it. It's only for a couple of months and then I'll be back and we'll be able to take care of those things. We'll get out of that dump where we've been living and move somewhere we've always wanted and build our lives…"

Her cloy words taper away as she walks out of the room. Oddly, everyone seems to pause from talking as she passes. Whatever she is doing, she certainly seems to get everyone's attention. Instantly, commentary fills the space of her departure.

"That lady gets on my nerves."

"Why?"

"She's always walking around announcing her business."

"Well then put your ear plugs in."

"Why do I have to adjust myself to compensate for her? I shouldn't have to plug my ears just to keep her cackling chatter out of my head. I shouldn't have to block out the whole world just to accommodate her. She isn't talking to anyone on the phone anyway. She's just another crazy person with all the other loonies that are crazy enough to come work at a job like this."

"Where else are you going to earn $6,000 in two months? You're here."

"But that doesn't mean I have to listen to her. I'm not paid to listen to her."

"Well I don't mind it."

"Well then maybe you two should hook up. Then she'd actually have a real person to talk to."

"You'd be surprised at the impact a passing word can have on a person's life."

"Yea, right."

"Let me tell you a story. I knew this one guy who was in Vietnam and when he came back he was assigned to do some public relations work for the Army at an Air Show. At one point they did a demonstration with a 20mm gun that completely caught him off guard. He was back home and he thought he was safe and all the sudden the world began to erupt with gunfire around him. He said all he could remember next was lying on the ground with his pistol drawn in the middle of the crowd. He could see the surrounding faces looking at him with the most terrified expressions. Just then a little old lady standing next to him said, 'You can get up now son.' He told me that he can still hear her voice with absolute clarity even to this day. That one phrase she made in the perfect tone, with the perfect words, at the perfect time completely deprogramed him from instinctively fighting for survival, so that he could return to a civil life. If what Carol says can help anyone, then I say let her talk all she wants. I'd rather hear a woman's reassuring voice, even if she isn't speaking to me, than hear nothing but these machines."

Nunatak

At dinner someone says we'll probably work until midnight. Back in the slime line, as soon as I start working, I fix my thoughts on the next break at 8 PM. The sense of a fixed goal sooths my unsettled thoughts. But then I consider what this break will entail. I will only have 15 minutes off, a short tease, and then I'll be back exactly where I am now. It feels hopeless.

I then decide to fix my thoughts on Midnight, the completion of the day. Then I consider going to sleep and waking up the next day. Again I end up in the same place, doing the same thing. I gain a sense of a relentless and ruthless routine leading nowhere. I actually begin to lose sympathy for the fish. Perhaps cutting them off from the mindless cycle of their lives is their salvation. Perhaps being served upon plates gives their lives an opportunity to broaden themselves in ways they could have never anticipated. Instead of simply spawning and dying upstream, the protein of their body may become the muscle fibers of someone building a bridge overlooking the stunning beauty of the Big Sur as traffic breezes past; it could piece into the excited neurons of a professor's mind lecturing on distant galaxies that spark stars in the eyes of attentive and aspiring students.

I recall Carol's passing comments from earlier and actual do find some reassurance in her words. She said the season will be over in a couple of months. I'll have a bundle of cash to do as I please. I will have a bolstering sense of accomplishment, even if it is only a demonstration of my endurance. I'll be cut free and released from a grueling season. It's not like I have to do this my entire life. It's not like I'm living in the Soviet Union where people had to work 14 hour days, 6 days a week in a factory for nothing. Then on their one free day a week, they would wait in bread lines. There were millions of people for several generations that were enslaved to that routine for their entire lives. All they had to look forward to was to die. It always puzzled me how a population can become so dissatisfied and disgusted with how a governing body mismanages their resources that they become convinced they should surrender all their resources, even the possession and direction of their own lives, to a governing body.

Then I compare this with my own situation. With the money this job provides, with the money I earn, what will I do? Will I just use it to run, to grease my wheels and spin off into the aimless velocity of laughing detachment? Will it just fuel more dazzling flames or will I use it to sustain something worth preserving? When this season is complete, I will be standing on top of a mountain. I have reached that peak before. I have stood at that ideal height where everything is within view, but nothing is within reach. From that peak every direction is open, every slope plunges in rolling momentum with the ease of opportunity. But every time I reach the base where I may make my own way, I find myself at what I'd abandoned before.   So I only turn to struggle up the desolate ascent again.

24

The next morning I'm back in the fish house. After the first hour, I feel a tap at my shoulder. "Hey big guy." I turn around. "Come with me."

Outside, he instructs me to take off my rain gear. He points to a door where we are to meet.

After peeling off my suit I step through the door. There is a line of ten huge tubes about 5 feet high and 60 feet long. They look like the old steam locomotives except without the wheels. A geyser of steam hisses toward the ceiling from a valve mounted on the top of one.

A guy with a clipboard walks over to me and asks my name.

"You've been re-assigned. You'll probably like this job too. It's dry. If you do well, we'll probably keep you here the entire season." Sounds good to me. He continues, "This is where we cook the cans of salmon. We load up the buggies and roll ten of them into each cooker." He hands me a pair of gloves and waves a guy over from one of the tables. "Sergio, this is Evan. He's going to be working with us. Get him going pushing the buggies and loading the cookers."

Sergio guides me to a table and as we walk, I watch another guy wheeling one of the buggies. He leans steeply into the load, obviously straining with the weight. Once the buggy is moving, he then wrestles to steer it toward a small steel rail bridge that crosses into one of the huge tube cookers. I watch him disappear as he pushes the buggy inside and then shortly after, rise from a his stoop from inside the tube and walks to ready himself by another buggy as it fills.

Sergio positions me at the end of one of the tables where a buggy is being loaded. The buggies look like big baskets on wheels, but instead of wicker, these baskets are made of iron. The buggies roll onto a small hydraulic lift at the end of the table where they are filled with layers of cans.

While I wait for the buggy to fill, Sergio explains that after the fish are cleaned in the fish house where I had been working, they are channeled into hoppers. These are small, funnel shaped storage containers that drop the fish into a filler. The filler is the machine that cuts the fish and crams them into cans. After the cans are filled, they are weighed. The cans that are light are channeled to another line that is called the patch table where workers add pieces of fish so that each can weighs a pound. Then the cans are spun through a seamer that caps and seals them. All this occurs in a continuous flow that gushes an uninterrupted rush of cans onto the table in front of me. As the table fills, two workers take a divisor and slide the number of cans to fill a layer in the buggy. As each layer is filled, the hydraulic lift lowers, a metal screen is set inside and another layer is slid on top the other until the buggy is full.

I count about two hundred cans in each layer and ten layers in each buggy. This amounts to 2000 cans. Since each can weighs a pound, each buggy holds a short ton of salmon. I can see why the guy was straining as he pushed the load.

When the buggy fills, Sergio asks if I'm ready. He shouts and we heave the buggy into motion and wheel it into the cooker. The buggy we push is the tenth which fills the cooker. He has me lift the steel bridge from the concrete platform and he closes the door. The lock is a wheel clamp similar to what one that would see on an old sea vessel where the doors could seal each chamber.

Sergio shouts to the supervisor, "el número 4, locked." The supervisor acknowledges with a thumbs up and adjusts some controls. Sergio points toward the empty buggies parked beyond the row of cookers. "Get another buggy ready for when this one is filled." The cans are turning out from the line at a steady stream rushing onto the table. Several layers of cans are slid onto a buggy every minute. They fill very quickly.

Sergio continues, "We're going really slow now. There are only two can lines running. When the pink really start coming in, then we'll have all six lines running and this place is hopping. All ten cookers are filled and the loaded buggies begin stacking up. If anyone makes a mistake and we fall behind, these cans start piling up on top of us until we're buried. I'll help you with this for a while and then I'll let you take over. After break, we'll get you loading the buggies too so you'll know how to work both sides of the job."

The work is straight forward. Soon I'm handling the buggies by myself. The strain in moving them is exhilarating. Knowing that I am the driving force behind a single ton is certainly more gratifying than standing around a revolving table cutting fins from fish. As I build my confidence in managing the full buggies, I wheel one into a cooker and build up some speed. It slams into the others inside and I hear the loud resonance of heavy metal reverberating through the tube. I feel like the full blown piston of a steam engine.

When I stand from my stoop outside the tube and feel myself flexing with pride, I notice Sergio staring at me with an infuriated expression. "Don't slam the buggies in the cooker."

I find his words a little hurtful as they bruise the sensitivity of my strength and I respond, "What am I going to break them? They're made of iron." What is he jealous? It's like a boxing trainer complaining that I might hurt my opponent, or perhaps someone concerned about me stepping in front of a freight train because I'll wreck the locomotive.

"No, the cans start bouncing out of the buggies and then jam up the wheels when they're pulled out." Sergio explains, "Do you want to try pushing one of these buggies without wheels? When you start getting reckless here, you start messing up and people get hurt. You don't want one of these buggies tipping over on the bridge or rolling over someone's foot. These things can snap bones like twigs."

My sense of exhilaration is immediately deflated. Of course he's right. I wasn't given this job to demonstrate my machismo. This is a job they thought I could handle. Strength can be an effective leverage, but without self-control, it's useless and dangerous.

Eventually, I've made the adjustments. I move the carts around like dainty tea cups at an English brunch. In my hands, they roll into the cooker swiftly and efficiently until they bump together with the gentlest kiss that would make tender love birds feel clunky and cumbersome in comparison. I settle into the job and soon I'm laughing and patting backs with the best of them. This may be on the other end of the line from the Fish House, but it feels a world away. I feel like I'm out of the bowels and into the open and fortunately my exit happened to be on the top side, not the bottom.

Garrett Buhl Robinson

25

Over the next few days the operations continue to accelerate as more volume is available to be processed. Eventually, all six can lines are running. The fish are pouring in as if the ocean was turned upside down at the top of the line. At this point, everyone knows what to do. Our motions mesh together as we move through the product like we are pulling the oars of a galley cruising through the season. At the other side of the cookers, I see the cans stacking in crates to be shipped to dinner tables all over the world.

I push two baskets at a time now. The thought of propelling two tons before me, not simply with strength, but with finesse, fills me with fire. As I lean into the weight, each step pushing from one foot to the other, I feel like I am plowing every reluctance and reservation out of my way. The ponderous burden of my life begins to float in the lofty velocity I achieve. I feel I am lifting myself upon powerful wings. I feel throttled like a rocket. I feel unstoppable.

I am not going back to Connie. There is no way. I can't. I shouldn't. I don't love her. I know she would stabilize my life. I know she would give me comfort. But what good is stability and comfort if it is built around discontent. I can't try to commit myself to something because of what it would provide me when I can't offer anything in return. All I've given her is empty promises, promises that I'll never fulfill. I can't keep doing that.

We work until midnight. There is still plenty of fish for tomorrow and more on the way. The season is in full swing. An ocean of Salmon is surging toward land, filling the rivers, filling the boats and filling the cans. I feel enlivened with work and purpose. I have made my decision. After the season I will be moving on. Do I know where I'm going? Of course not. If I knew where, I would have already been there and then what would be the purpose in going? I have to be honest with Connie and with myself. It's not fair leading her on with my indecisiveness. I have to be firm. I have to show my resolve. I have to end it.

The next day, I write her a letter during the breaks. The opening is "Dearest Constance, there are a million reasons why I should marry you, but not one of them is love and without that, does anything else really matter?" The rest of the letter is filled with explanations and each line begins with "I can't" until I finally say goodbye and sign my name. I hesitate in sealing the letter. Her birthday is approaching and she will probably think the letter is a happy wish, instead of a heartbreak.

This is the right decision though. This is the strong choice to make. It would be weak to keep her hanging on hoping for something I cannot give. I am just dangling her beneath me like a safety net. It is far more cruel to keep baiting her along thinking there is some possibility, that there is some chance, when there is not. She said she would wait for me to return and then she would tell me that she would marry me. It's selfish of me to keep her waiting if I can't make the commitment. It is better to break it off than to keep dragging her behind me as if I don't notice her there and don't care. I do care, just not in the way I need to, not in the way she deserves.

I seal the envelope and drop it in the box. It is done. I return to work. I can't wait to finish this season and make my escape from this place. After working in this can, anywhere will be a refreshment.

That evening, just 15 minutes before midnight, I'm pushing two buggies into a cooker. While I'm deep inside I notice the light dim. I stop in my tracks and look back. Someone is pushing a buggy in behind me. I'm going to be smashed between them and then my broken body will be cooked alive before anyone notices. I begin to yell, "Hold up, I'm in here." The buggy keeps approaching. "Hold up! Stop!" I then hear people outside begin to yell too and the buggy slows and begins backing out. What an idiot. Fortunately the others outside noticed.

I turn back to the two buggies I was pushing. They have come to a complete stop. From inside the cooker, pushing two buggies back into motion is a challenge. I lean into the weight, my arms stretched out over my head and I strain to budge the dead weight. They begin to roll. Suddenly, my foot slips and I fall forward. To keep from smashing my face on the metal rail, I try catching myself on the buggy but the weight of my body drags me down and I feel my left shoulder pop out of its socket. I slip to a knee as the buggies roll away and clack to a stop. A searing pain shoots through my arm and an excruciating flame of sensation licks the inside of my head. It feels like I broke my arm. My shoulder then slips back into the socket. I feel a surge of more pain as I realize I have broken my body beneath my own weight.

I stagger outside. Lifting my head outside the tube, I realize I can't move my arm. It drops limp and useless. Everyone is pointing and laughing at me. They have no idea about my shoulder. They think me almost being trapped inside between the buggies is funny. They yell for me to bring another empty buggy. I walk to the retrieve one, but I can't even lift my left arm to set on the edge of the basket, let alone to exert any effort to push, even with the basket being empty. I push it with one arm, constantly having to counter on each side as it rolls in a weaving line of alternating compensations. Just a moment ago I was flaring my nostrils while I pushed two loaded carts and now I can't even manage an empty one. Fortunately midnight arrives and the lines shut down before I need to move another cart. The supervisor announces for everyone to be back at eight o'clock tomorrow morning. Everyone disperses. As I walk away, gingerly cradling my left arm against my body, I realize even the thought of lifting my arm sends excruciating pain up from my shoulder.

Nunatak

Not only will my shoulder not let me work, that night, I find it will not let me sleep either. I definitely can't lie on my left side, but even lying on my right sight aggravates the injury. Lying on my stomach is excruciating. The best I can do is lie on my back and take shallow breaths. I don't know what I'm going to do in the morning. I feel like all the salmon for my season have been dumped on the floor and I am sinking in rotting carcasses as everything goes to waste. I eventually do sleep some through the night. I know this because of the numerous times I wake in teeth gritting pain from my body unconsciously shifting around. My entire night becomes a strobe of exhausted oblivion repeatedly roused with searing pain.

Garrett Buhl Robinson

26

The next morning I arise from bed and walk to the worksite. I still can't lift my arm. The pain is one matter, but despite the pain, the swelling has immobilized the joint. This is something beyond my own will. My left arm simply does not work. For all practical purposes, it is detached from my conscious mind, with the exception of the pain receptors. My body has taken it out of action to allow it to heal.

Arriving at the work site, I approach the supervisor. Initially he is happy to see me, but I can see his expression quickly sour as I approach. Obviously he can read the expression of dejected defeat on my face. Coddling my arm against my body, I am the walking wounded. I tell him that I hurt my arm last night and I can't do this job anymore. It would be impossible. He asks if I can load the buggies. He wants to work with me on this. I just shake my lowered head. I have to see the nurse at the clinic.

While I'm walking out, everyone thinks I quit. Someone shouts, "You scared of getting cooked?" Apparently they think that last night's incident when I was nearly trapped in the cooker between buggies is my concern. That's the least of my worries though. I don't bother explaining. They can think what they want. Now I have to figure out how I can salvage this season. We haven't even received our first pay check, and I already feel null and void.

I walk to the stock room to inquire about the clinic. I haven't the faintest idea where it is or when it opens. Out on the docks, the crowds that I am accustomed to are gone. Everyone is busy at work. My shoulder has been dislodged from the socket. I am dislodged from the job. My running leap to wherever I please after the Salmon season has stumbled before I even picked up speed and the fat cushion of cash I was imagining has vanished and I am falling fast. Yesterday, I was moving the world before me. Today, I am like a helpless fish ensnared in a net of my own nerves.

The clinic doesn't open until 9 AM. I sit outside partially covered by an overhang. I am still bundling my arm against my body. I don't know what else to do with it. The rain falls on my pants that extend from beneath the cover. The water soaks the fabric and pronounces the sharp, dry line from the exposed length of my legs.

When the nurse arrives I wait in line. When the nurse sees me, he suspects I am right about the dislocated shoulder. He asks me to try lifting my arm and I can only nudge it from my torso like a broken flipper. There is no range of motion. There is no functionality. There is only a dangling piece of meat and bone that can do nothing but hurt.

He gives me a couple ibuprofen tablets. I tell him that I have to work. I can still use my right arm. I plead if he can have me assigned somewhere. He sends me to the stock room.

Nunatak

In the stock room, I am graciously given an assignment of filling freezer bags. Each bag is filled with some mysterious fluid that is frozen and packaged with the fish from Cold Storage for shipping. During the break, as people line up for supplies, I feel the weight of staring eyes watching me in the back as I perform my cushy job. I feel weak, as if this simple task is all I can handle, and for the time being, apparently it is. I feel humiliated and hopeless. I feel like I'm in a laughing stock. Of course, it is absurd to think anyone recognizes me. Hundreds of people work here. Trying to dismiss what I feel on the basis of anonymity is useless though. This shame is not in their opinions; this shame is in myself.

While I'm working I keep considering the coincidence of sending the letter to Connie and dislocating my shoulder. I think of Karma. I don't believe in Karma though. I refuse to believe that my only motivation for treating other people well is from some fear of supernatural retribution, as if I am some lab rat driven through a maze by punishment and reward. I try to make the best decisions not because I think some god will punish me, but because I do not want to disrupt other people's lives. I am not being cruel to Connie by sending that letter. The selfish decision would be to have her wait for me, to claim a commitment which I'm not willing to fulfill, to lift her with lofty promises that I can't live up to.

I'm doing the right thing. I'm making the tough choice. I'm breaking it off before it goes too far and we're both entangled in something neither of us really want. I'm giving her a chance to find someone else. She's a beautiful lady and a beautiful person. She has a gracious personality. She won't have any problem finding someone else. She doesn't need to get hung up on me, not when I'll only let her down. Plus, I'm teaching her an invaluable lesson. I'm teaching her the futility of misplacing her affections and love on a person like me.

Yes, she may be hurt when she receives the letter, but I'm hurt too. I'm emotionally torn. I have been since I left. I've been torn by not letting myself go. Now I'm in excruciating pain. But I'm not going to crawl back to her now because I'm hurt. If that is my reason, then what will I do when I heal? Like I told myself before, she would be helpful for my life, but I don't need her. I don't need anyone. I will make it through this. I don't care if I have to crawl. I don't care if I have to drag my body by clawing at the floor with my one good arm. I'm not giving up. I'm not giving in. I'll pick myself up again. I'll get back on my feet. This isn't the first problem in life I've encountered. This isn't the end. This is just another obstacle. This is just another opportunity for me to demonstrate my persistence. This isn't the first challenge I have surmounted in my life.

If there is any connection between my injury and that letter, it could only be weakness. The hesitation I felt about sending it, the uncertainty from the sticky, sappy sense of sentimentality must have tripped me up. I was looking back while I was moving forward. That is what caused me to stumble and fall on my face with a broken shoulder. I don't have time for superstitions. I don't have time for silly gimmicks. I'm not going to try to explain my life by some celestial fantasy. I guide my life by reason and in this case, in regards to Connie, I am making the right decision, the strong and sure decision. This is just another simple hang-up, another minor snag that I will break myself away from. There is no looking back, there is only the task at hand, even if right now, I only have one hand. I must work with what I have. That's what I know and that's what I do, and I'll do it until it's done. And that is all there is to it.

I maintain this discourse in my head for hours while I fill each little bag with some mysterious, clear, gelatinous chemical that holds the cold from a refrigerant. As I fill each bag from a long sleeve of plastic on a roller, I use a heat pad to make the seal. The bags look like the ones you'd carry from a pet store and I keep expecting to see a goldfish floating in one, looking out through a strangely blurred lens into an indistinct and distant world it is jostled and carried through. I drop each sealed bag into an accumulating pile inside a large, cardboard box on the floor. I hear the plop of each one flop on the others like I'm filling a tote with synthetic salmon.

At 5 PM, a lady who works in the stock room walks into the back. "You can't get any overtime doing this. You know just we're letting you do this to help you out." She looks down into the box and says, "We don't really need all these bags anyway." She suddenly walks back into the front. I can hear her tell the others about all the bags I made in the back. She then returns and tells me I have to move that box out of their way before I leave.

27

The next morning I walk to Cold Storage. Perhaps the supervisor will be sympathetic and find an assignment that will allow me to work around my injury. I arrive in my rain gear knowing that I am less likely to be refused if I show up dressed for work, if not completely ready physically. Finding one of the supervisors, I explain my situation. My right arm is fully functional and I can manage using my left arm below the elbow. As long as I don't have to lift my arm, I can work fairly well at waist level.

The supervisor leads me toward the beginning of the processing line. He installs me in front of a short conveyer belt that branches off the main line and spins a short distance toward a drain. A constant rinse of water splashes down the drain's dark hole. The whistle sounds and the machinery is kicked into gear. The engine of the fork lift revs as a tote is lifted and tipped to pour gallons of fish onto the top of the line. At the station I have been positioned, I stand by two ladies who speak in Spanish while we wait. As the fish begin to sort down the line, piles of entrails emerge on the tiny belt in front of me. The ladies pick up the entrails and tear away the sacks of eggs. They set the clusters of bright orange roe in plastic baskets and the entrails drop down the drain.

Easy enough. The sacks tear away without any resistance. They do not cling like the fins to the body or the muscles to the bones. The eggs give way with the gentlest tugs; they were made to be released; they evolved for dispersion. I position a stack of baskets beside me, reach and grab a cluster of eggs with my right hand, lift them to my left to tear them apart and then set the eggs in the basket. Since I am not able to reach out with my left hand, I cannot keep pace with the ladies. At times, expressions of disappointment cross their faces as disgusted scowls. They must compensate for my lag. They must lift me and my slack in addition to their own load. Still, I busily tear through globs of viscera, working as quickly as I can. Several times I find myself wincing with the pain in my shoulder, but I wonder if this is from aggravating my injury or trying to indicate my infirmary and excuse my poor performance.

At one point the lady across from me grabs the same clump of viscera and eggs that I grab. Politely, I immediately acquiesce and release the clump so that I may not interfere with her work. She sneers in disgust. The exact opposite reaction I was expecting from my thoughtful decision. I don't speak Spanish, or rather I don't know any Spanish that I can express in a genteel way, so there is no chance to ask for an explanation of what I am doing wrong. All I can do is continue working as diligently as I can as my hands scramble through offal.

In our frenzy to keep up with the conveyer belt the lady and I grab the same clump of viscera again. This time, instead of politely acquiescing, I grip the viscera more firmly and try ripping the clump from her hand as if in spite of her disapproval from before. As I do this, the sack of roe and the viscera tear away between us. I find that what I was doing with my own two hands, could also be done between us and increase our efficiency and effectiveness in working together. This is what she must have meant when she expressed her disappointment before. It was like playing paddy-cakes where one claps one's hands together and then claps them with the hands of the others as the melody revolves in a working circle, or like giving a high five with a team member in a leaping ovation by applauding one another with each other's hands.

For the next two days, I work in this same position. Eventually I am able to move back to the cold storage line and spoon as I had done before. The operation allows me to use my left arm minimally, simply opening the flaps of the fish's sliced bellies while my right hand works the spoon and suction tube through the abdominal cavity. No doubt my body complains with pain, but I can function and I work through it, hopefully without causing permanent damage. I even feel a sense of pride in the fact that despite a dislocated shoulder, I only missed a couple of hours of work. I feel more exhilaration from this than pushing the buggies. Moving massive objects and pushing weight around is one thing, but negotiating obstacles and overcoming difficulties is another. It is not a reckless path narrowing as it barrels down steepening slopes, plunging to smash at the bottom; it is a thoughtful exhilaration, full of assured momentum and guided with widely awakened attention.

28

That night at dinner I'm sitting with my regular crowd. Through time, Tuesday has begun to loosen up while talking with the rest of the group. This seemed to coincide with the receipt of our first check upon which he promptly repaid me. Tonight he actually opens the conversation with the question, "Has anyone noticed that the processing lines are very similar to a digestive track?"

Everyone responds, not by speaking, but by momentarily pausing from chewing their food to ruminate over this in their minds. I envision a textbook diagram of the digestive track in my head. I see the shaded figure of a human form and sketch the drawing of the esophagus leading to the pink colored sack of the stomach. Then my mind twists through the sinuous course of the small intestines until they broaden into the colon that encircles the interior of the abdomen. With this complete image of the alimentary canal, I try superimposing it upon the image of the processing line as I reassemble it in my mind. I turn the images in different ways as I try to find an overlapping match, hoping to recognize in what way they align.

Tuesday continues, "It's like a means of ingesting the fish into the economy for the sustenance of the population. The fish house is like the masticating of chewing. Then the fish continue through the conveyers, circulating through the system, until they are packed in cans just like molecules bound together in fatty cells for storage. This whole place is like one devouring mouth of society, partially digesting the food to be circulated through the market and distributed through the population that all together composes the body of society."

It is an interesting analogy. I must admit that while he is making the explanation, I am still attempting to match the overlapping images in my head. I think of the numerous drains I have stared into. The clocks have even begun to resemble the drains, their arms whirling like the swirling water on their changeless, gaping faces. "What about the drains. Where do all the pieces of fish go?"

"The Reduction plant. Nothing is thrown away. The fish heads and the viscera are processed, packaged and sold as pet food."

Soon, we're all walking back to the plant. We stick together until we reach the dock and then we veer off to our own separate assignments.

29

For the next five weeks the boats continue to bring a steady stream of fish. We work every day of the week from 8 AM until midnight. Some people work even longer days. Every day is buried beneath another layer of fatigue that is broken with nothing more than insensible blinks of sleep. I have never before experienced the reality of lying down in bed and falling asleep before my head hits the pillow, until now. In fact, it seems that before my head hits the pillow my alarm clock goes off and it is time to arise for another day of work. Some people actually wake and see the conveyer belt running across the ceiling of their bunk bed. The repetition of the images becomes emblazed in our thoughts. Fish begin to swim behind the lids of our closed eyes and spawn in the thoughts of our minds. Cogged along the conveyer, our minds begin to work in the same procedure as the line's process. Our plastic minds reshape in the forms of our engagements.

My life and outlook have become fixed upon one single alignment and that is the alignment of the hour and minute hand of the clock at midnight that marks the completion of each work day. At that alignment I know I have the sweet refreshment of rest to look forward to. And even if that rest is practically a non-existent instance that eludes my consciousness, it is a sweet dip into oblivion. That sight of alignment becomes the finish line, the place I pace myself upon, the golden goal on which I fix my future. It's not high noon; it's the deepest recess of the night, but it is the place I touch bottom and from where I may push off to surge back to the surface.

Some days, the clock reaches midnight and the line continues to run. It is like reaching for that destination, lunging through that last stretch, only to find the goal receding and taunting from an evasive distance. That nadir of the night, that bottom I had hoped to reach and push up from suddenly opens and swallows me whole. That marker, as arbitrary as it may be, is the treasure of significance I give it, and with all the attention I pour upon it, when it is gone, when it is rendered as nothing, I am left staggering in a vacancy, tumbling in a void, languishing in limbo, dissipating in the illusion I project. When that sparkling moment becomes just another bloody increment in an endless and relentless line of slaughter, I lose all bearing in life. With that one fixed sense of completion removed, I feel my whole life depleting into an unfulfilling emptiness.

30

The season does end though. In early September the cannery closes but cold storage stays open. There are still fish to be processed, but different fish. Other places I've lived are marked with seasons of the year. Here it seems to be seasons of fish. The Salmon have past. Cod and Halibut begin to arrive. Unlike Salmon though, there is no overwhelming glut. There is no need for the massive work force. Suddenly, most everyone is gone.

On a Saturday night, I am sitting with the group at dinner. It is the last night the cafeteria is open. Everyone is flying out the next day except for me.

Lynn asks me, leaning against Ross who has his arm over her shoulder while he talks with Lee, "How long are you staying Evan?"

"I don't know."

"Don't you have someone to go back to?"

"No." I lie, or rather, I continue tearing myself apart as I try to make the statement true. I quickly change the subject, "When are you two getting married?"

When I ask this, Ross stops talking and him and Lynn turn toward each other and stare deeply into one another's eyes. After a moment they both turn to look at me as if responding together, "As soon as we get back. Really we've been married all our lives, we just didn't realize it until a year ago. The whole reason for the trip is to pay for the marriage and have some money to move into a new place."

"I think that's great," Lee adds. "I don't think I've ever seen two people more in love."

Ross says, "Something for certain, for the rest of my life, I'm going to make sure that Lynn knows she is the luckiest lady in the world. We may struggle through some days, and I'm sure we will, but each day will end, as each day will begin, with us together forever."

"Yes, it is truly a beautiful thing," Tuesday adds. "I can't think of anything more wonderful for two people than to share their lives together."

Lynn changes the direction of the conversation abruptly, "Tuesday, I have a question for you since you seem to know practically everything. What do you think of same sex marriage?"

"I think marriage is more than about sex. It's a lifetime commitment, a commitment between two people to share their lives together. It is the most intimate and trusting relationship through which two people may nurture a life beyond themselves, beyond what they could ever be alone. The sanctity of marriage is not in people's opinions or in a group's consent or an institution's decree. The sanctity of marriage is within the marriage itself, within the union between two individuals and if two people are in love, who would come between them?"

160

Nunatak

The more they discuss marriage, the more excluded I feel from the conversation, the stronger my sense of betrayal of Connie.

31

The next day, I catch Tuesday before he leaves. He is sitting outside by himself. I approach him, "Tuesday, can I ask you a question?"

He looks up at me curiously, "You just did."

I pause for a second, "Oh yea, I guess so. What're you doing?"

"Just organizing information in my head. Why? Is that what you wanted to ask?"

"No, it's just that while I've gotten to know you over the last couple of months, I have begun to hold your ideas and opinions at high regard, although I must admit I don't always grasp them completely. But I was wondering, what do you think gives life meaning?"

"The meaning of our lives is not in ourselves, it is in our relations."

"But what about in general. What about life as a whole."

"The meaning of life is to survive and that can only be done together, through diversity, through the past, through the future, through the present. Life lives."

That evening, I find everyone from the group has gone. The next morning, I slip into my rain gear and clean cod. The work days are shorter, eight hours or less, but it gives me something to do; it keeps me engaged; it provides an anchor upon which I circle from the length of a chain from one day to the next until I figure out what I will do, which way I will wander, in which direction I will disappear in the fading image of myself. From the processing line, I look out into life like I look out of the gaping doors of this warehouse. I see rain; I feel the cold.

Two days later I receive another check, my last big check from the Salmon season. I now have well over $6000. I have enough cash to go practically anywhere I want. I can just pick a city. I know the routine. I find a job. I build myself up again and then I give it all away. I am standing on the top of the mountain again, that ideal peak where everything is in view, but nothing is within reach.

This time is different though. I have found that I am not Sisyphus; I am Sisyphus' rock. I push away from every approach because I remain as closed as a stone. I never turn toward anything because I am only turning away, smashing and crashing in the leaps of every fall, throwing sparks as I crumble, grinding myself into gravel.

I look at the deposit receipt again and stare at the number. I see the bills flying away as I buy food, pay rent, and squander trifles. The digits always revolve to zero again. Then I think of the hardest rock. Not granite, not my heart, but carbon, a diamond sparkling and flashing with dazzling facets of lapidary magnificence. I see it on a tender finger of a supple hand extending with two open arms and I see Connie, smiling. I don't see a zero. I see a ring. I don't see a lifetime of loneliness. I see a lifetime of love. Like dawn on the horizon, like brightening day, I see my lonely heart is not incomplete, it is not un-whole, it is simply closed. The reason I have never felt love and the reason I have never had any love to give, is because I have never accepted love.

****

Made in the USA
Charleston, SC
21 November 2012